S0-CFG-411

SHAMELESS

Women's Intimate
Erotica

SHAMELESS

Women's Intimate Erotica

EDITED BY HANNE BLANK

SEAL PRESS

SHAMELESS: WOMEN'S INTIMATE EROTICA

Seal Press
An Imprint of Avalon Publishing Group Inc.
161 William St., 16th Floor
New York, NY 10038

Collection copyright © 2002 by Seal Press
First Seal Press edition 2002

Book design by Paul Paddock

"Persistence of Memory" © 2002 by Catherine Lundoff
"The Fourteenth Day" © 2002 by L.E. Bland
"Cages" © 2002 by Simone Temple
"Perfect" © 2002 by Helena Grey
"A Cool Dry Place" © 2002 by R. Gay
"Communion" © 2002 by Jean Roberta
"The Book of Zanah" © 2002 by Anne Tourney
"Pregnant Pause" © 2002 by Dawn O'Hara
"Lust, Debt and a Practical Education" © 2002 by Hanne Blank
"Spark Me" © 2002 by Jessica Melusine
"Stone Cold *(A Confession)*" © 2002 by Zonna
"When We Were One" © 2002 by Helena Settimana
"To Remember You By" © 2002 by Sacchi Green
"Deeper" © 2002 by Jaclyn Friedman
"I Can Still Smell You" © 2002 by Lucy Moore
"Seven Women" © 2002 by Hua Tsao Mao
"Swell" © 2002 by Heather Corinna
"Dear Nicholas" © 2002 by Adhara Law

All rights reserved. No part of this book may be reproduced in whole
or in part without written permission from the publisher.

Library of Congress Cataloging-in-Publication Data is available.

ISBN: 1-58005-060-3

Printed in the United States of America
Distributed by Publishers Group West

contents

Acknowledgments

Perhaps it's obvious when the book in question is an anthology, but creating a book is definitely not a solo endeavor. I'd like to publicly acknowledge the help, support, inspiration, and all-around wonderfulness not only of the writers who contributed to this book, but also to the following individuals who deserve special commendation for their role in making me possible while I was doing the same for this book: My co-conspiratrix Heather Corinna and the staff at *Scarlet Letters*, Princess Warrior of Perky Deb Malkin, the ever-uppity Dr. Gil Rodman, mom extraordinaire Shanna Spalding, spondoolix foodie queen Liz Tamny, Lisa "Bou Galoux" Williams *et les snooches galantes*, the *Sojourner* Pussy Posse, and my wonderful editor at Seal Press, Leslie Miller. A shameless lot, indeed.

Hanne Blank

Introduction

When we think about the sex that really fires us, the stuff that puts a quiver in our bellies and slick wetness between our legs, our minds go in one of two directions. Sometimes they take us swiftly forward to the wishful thinking of classic fantasy, immaculate projections unsullied by the myriad little imperfections of real, complicated bodies, personalities, and emotions. Fantasizing means thinking big: scenarios, positions and acts, idealized situations and bodies, all of it exactly the way we imagine that we want it most.

In the other direction, we head back into our cache of memories, sifting through to find the recalled images, sensations, and scenes that send bright sparks of arousal spinning into our increasingly rushing blood. But sexual memory works on a very different scale than sexual fantasy. Memory depends on little things, interior things, detail and texture, taste and smell, how we felt, what we noticed, how body met body. We recall the hues of light on skin, the ache of an overtaxed muscle, the heat of a blush, the feeling of fumbling artlessly with a zipper or bra clasp. Erotic memory is not so much about the ways we want it most, but the ways we've gotten it best. It resurrects the critical details that anchor our arousal, touching us in the most intimate places, where priceless juxtapositions of sensation, thought, and emotion are inscribed indelibly into our flesh.

This book is an effort to marry these two ways of thinking about sex, to merge the flexibility of fantasy with the physicality and intimacy of memory. Hence, the theme of the collection has nothing to do with content—no theme in the sense of the stories all relating to a single topic, or a single type of sexuality—but everything to do with style. Memoir after memoir fills this book, but the memoir here is an illusion, a *trompe l'oeil*. Regardless of how they may appear, the stories contained in this volume are fictional.

Or are they? I like to think that they are real stories of real people— women who happen to exist only because they have stories to tell.

And what a bunch of stories they are. Despite the fact that this is a book of erotica, the thing that links the stories in this book to one another is not the fact that their narrators have lots of sex. What links the stories and their narrators, what makes them so compelling isn't that they fuck but that they fuck with passion, with attitude, with deep emotion . . . and with fascinating, often searingly erotic, insight. Memoir-style storytelling brings it all into focus, a heady, richly-scented bouillabaisse of detail, a luscious, unabashed chorus of women who regale us with memories whose flavor we somehow seem to recognize, no matter how far those memories may be from our own.

This is one of the delights of memoir—it lets us in. It gives us a vantage point from which to know the storyteller in intimate ways, from the same perspective, and seemingly the same closeness, as we know ourselves. And many of these women are, indeed, like us. They are office workers (R. Gay's "A Cool Dry Place") and small-town librarians (Anne Tourney's "The Book of Zanah"), coffeeshop proprietors (Heather Corinna's "Swell") and nurses (Sacchi Green's "To Remember You By"). Between each set of unprepossessing sheets we find that the quality of a woman's sex life isn't about her clothes or her looks or her weight or her wealth, but about her soul and her enthusiasm, her emotional investment, her history, her openness to lust and pleasure and willingness to find it in places that may seem unorthodox, unlikely, even blasphemous. And on the rare occasion that we are introduced to a more stereotypical sex icon, such as the redhead exotic-dancer narrator of Simone Temple's

"Cages", we find that far from being the vapid caricature that traditional porn might lead us to expect, she too is multilayered, smart, self-aware, learning about herself and the world through sex and desire.

More to the point, she—and many of the other women in this book—reveal a sexuality that is distinctively female. After decades of necessary fight against the oppressive equation of physiology and destiny, it is only slowly becoming permissible for women to talk about how our bodies, and the specific aspects of our bodies and biology that make us female, affect and shape us and particularly our sexual selves. The perennial issue of sex during menstruation, for instance, raises its age-old head in Jean Roberta's "Communion." Fears, fantasies, and realities of conception and pregnancy form the nucleus of a pair of taboo-tapping and disarmingly candid tales, Dawn O'Hara's "Pregnant Pause" and L. E. Bland's "The Fourteenth Day," stories likely to resonate right where it counts . . . with more women than might ever want to admit it.

This is not to confuse the female with the feminine. Women *can* be feminine, but that's only one of the options. The real protagonist of Zonna's "Stone Cold," for instance, is butchness. In this story, as so often in real life, desperate lust and conquistador, cherry-busting sex are not enough to hide the vulnerability and fierce, sometimes vicious pride with which many masculine women negotiate the difficult outsider-ness of their gender niche. On the femme fatale end of the spectrum we find sexual revenge, that most unladylike motivation, slowly revealed as the core of Catherine Lundoff's obsessively carnal "Persistence of Memory." Then, demonstrating that none of these things are monolithic in any of our sexual personae, Hua Tsao Mao's "Seven Women" offers glimpses of seven very different affairs and seven different contexts of scalding sexual interaction—exploration, aggression, grief, submission, territorialism, and more—in a single woman's life.

These are, without question, some seriously sexy stories of women with profound, deeply carnal sides to their lives. Whether they are embracing the healing powers of sexual acceptance and desire, as in Helena Grey's "Perfect" (or, in a very different way, Jaclyn Friedman's "Deeper"), revisiting a lost love like the one in Lucy Moore's "I Can Still

Smell You," or simply having an all-out good and goofy time for the sake of the joy that's in it—as do the three kitsch-loving partners of Heather Corinna's "Swell"—these are women who love their sex. I mean that not just in the sense that they love engaging in sexual activity, but that they love their sex, too: they celebrate their bodies, their seductiveness, their breasts and clits, their ability to attract, their sexual capacity, their ability to revel in a ripe variety of pleasures that extends well beyond superficiality and stereotype. Both the stories and the women who tell them are shameless, in the very best sense of the word.

Yes, they're shameless, and they know Scheherazade's secret: that a vivid tale that carries its own sensual truths is a seduction all its own. And ravishing seductions they are, as redolent and physical in their detail as our most cherished individual moments of sensual recall, as pregnant with promise as the shiniest of our barely formed fantasies of what might someday be.

It is my hope as the editor that, as you read through these stories, you will allow them to tug at you, let them set up sympathetic vibrations that resonate with your own memories and fantasies. Let their gloriously messy, intrepid sexiness sink in. Long after the book is closed, I hope that the echoes linger to remind you that your own life is no less rich, no less voluptuous, than the lives in this book. It isn't in the way you look, or the number and type of partners you have, the sex acts you engage in, or the ones that you don't. Rather, it is in how you view it, what you bring to it, what you embrace, what you take away.

I hope that you will join me, and the other women in this book, writers and protagonists alike, in celebrating the rich mixture of experience and fantasy, desire and insight, the heat of the moment and the cool remove of days gone by. I hope that you too will insist on the vitality and beauty of the sexual in your own life . . . that you, too, will join the subversive, luscious ranks of the shameless.

Hanne Blank
October 2001
Columbia, Maryland

FOR MALCOLM K. GIN

For many years, I wondered at the fact that so many authors and editors dedicate their books to their life partners. Then I began to write and edit books of my own, and promptly discovered the reasons why. Thank you for gracing my work and my life.

SHAMELESS

Women's Intimate Erotica

Catherine Lundoff

PERSISTENCE OF MEMORY

Tonight, I'm all alone and dreams sit at my shoulder whispering the nasty thoughts that I write down. Their little tongues caress the edges of my mind as I remember how it used to be.

You are here with me tonight, your hands burning on my skin, your tongue probing, tasting me. I want it that way now, just like I did then. Why did you leave? For the moment, I forget.

Of course, I'll remember tomorrow. That's what my journal and my friends are for, endlessly helping me remember all the nights I missed you. The difference is that now I only have the longing, the screaming want between my legs that calls for you. Calls? Did I say calls? Let's not even think about that, about your voice on the line rubbing against me until I hump the receiver, the couch, anything I can find.

Tonight, I think of turning for comfort to those little metal balls in their velvet case. Do you remember when you bought them for me? I'll never forget it. You slipped them inside me, their icy touch making me shiver. Then you made me keep them in when we went to La Strada. You did it just to watch me squirm through my moussaka, the chair soaking beneath me and my breath coming in little gasps. Then you went back later and fucked the waitress.

I could have accepted that, if only you had invited me along for the ride. She had lovely lips, and with your little steel friends rubbing their way out of me, I wanted to taste their Jungle Red elegance. I wanted her to trail them over my naked breasts, see my nipples drawn up between them. Feel first you, then her inside me. Feel my clit sing against lips and tongue and hands, lots of hands. Feel my body shake itself to pieces when I came.

But no, I was left out of this, as with so many of your other pleasures. Why did you have to have Mark, just to name another? He was the only boss I ever liked. After you, his eyes traveled over me like an undiscovered landscape and I had to guess at what you had told him. Was it about what we did together? Or maybe what it took to make me come? Was that it?

I can no longer distinguish between what I wanted you to do and what you actually did. No matter. I had to leave that job or have him, too. I needed to know what you saw in him. I wanted it to rub off on me. I wanted to feel his rock-hard dick between my breasts, then between my thighs, exploring the source of the ancient rivers that flow inside me. His tongue riding the waves that rolled down from my pussy at the thought of his touch. At your/his/their fingertips roaming across my body.

If I try hard, I can picture how we met. It was at that seedy bar down on 54th. Malone's, I think. You were there with your friends and I was there with mine. Your eyes rode over, then under my dress, like little hands. I have never been so publicly undressed. You could have had me then, for the taking. Instead, we dated, courting in the old style. You kissed only my lips on our first date, but your touch stayed with me for days afterward.

We had so much in common, or so I thought at the time. We went to the art museum to hear some saxophone player you'd heard of. I can't recall her name, but the resonance of sax against marble was lovely. Your profile against that same marble was even lovelier. After that, there was nothing left but to think of you constantly, imagining all the while what it would be like to have you in my bed.

Your face burned its way onto the back of my eyelids until I saw you every time I closed my eyes. Your hands hadn't even begun to caress me in the waking world, but I could feel them on me when I tried to sleep. Vampire-like, you hovered outside the window in my dreams while I begged you to come in, displaying myself before you like a tasty meal. But I got only chaste kisses and rare phone calls for those agonizing weeks.

The night came when we went to the erotic poetry slam at that bar downtown. It was our third date, and by then it was hard to see through the steam rising off us, or at least off me. You held my hand while we listened to words about desire, love gone bad, lost loves. No one ever writes poetry about happy love. Who could relate? My pen trembles against the page as I remember you and consider the sonnet, the sestina. What could do justice to you? I sink back into my memories instead.

That night, your knee gently brushed against mine under the table and I shivered in delight. Your breath danced against my ear when you whispered to me, and I purred. I can't even remember what you said, only the warm comfort of your voice and the gleam in your eyes. Their dark brown sheen melted like chocolate on my breasts, in my mouth, at the edge of my hearing, until you were the only one in that bar. The tide of voices rose and fell around us as I looked first into your eyes and then at your hands.

Have you ever really thought about hands? Yours in particular, I mean. Those short, stubby fingers, the palms scarred and callused from work. Nothing special at first glance, those hands. But once you got to know them, they took on a strange elegance. So quick to learn, so adventurous in their wanderings, so clever in coaxing the reaction you wanted from whomever you touched.

That night I was both fascinated and repelled by them. You had paint under your broken nails. I wondered if your fingers would bruise my delicate skin when you came. I dared to hope they would and I wriggled closer until my thigh burned against yours. You smiled like a sleepy cat and spoke to me of Nicaraguan poets, of the slams at the Nuyorican Poets Cafe. I told you about Berlin as I slipped my foot out of my mule to stroke it along your ankle.

3

Your eyes were warm, kindly pools of indifference. I fell in, drowned, and asked you back to my place. Your silence filled up with cigarette smoke and noise from the surrounding tables until I was ready to crawl away. Then you stood, pulling me up and out the door with you. I barely had time to grab my purse and wave at your friends. They didn't seem to notice and I should have seen that, but right then all I saw was you.

We left in your car, your hand darting back and forth between the stick shift and my thigh. I straddled it finally, just so I could feel those dangerous little fingers slide up between my legs. By the time we got to my building, I would have cheerfully ridden the damn thing if I thought I could get through to you. Instead, you purred at me in Spanish, phrases that I barely understood. What were you saying to me that night? I answered in broken German and the frenzied syllables of my breasts and hips. English was too weak, too cold for what I wanted to say to you.

But then, words were never really what connected us, were they? They rolled down your tongue and straight into my pussy until a single look, a phrase made me drip in anticipation. I changed the way I dressed, embracing the zippered leather skirts and stockings with garters that you loved. I bought a black leather bustier and red lace push-up bras. I wore heels and even shaved my legs, all for you. At night some of the people in the places we went would watch me like I was already coated in whipped cream, in honey, and I warmed to their gaze.

Mostly, they watched you. There was one time at the club you liked when a woman in the bathroom pressed me up against the sink and kissed me, her lips and pierced tongue owning me for an instant. Her girlfriends dragged her out, laughing while I stood frozen, watching the metal door slam behind her. When I came back out, she was sitting in my chair, her lips at your ear. You shook your head, but I saw the way you watched her walk away.

It was that look that I saw so often, the gaze of a predator owning what it saw with single-minded intensity. I could not have withstood its burning heat if constancy had flared within it along with the lust and the calculation. I knew there would always be others, but I longed to be the primary, not the sole, object of that gaze. Sometimes I was, sometimes I wasn't. Sometimes I just couldn't tell. It was the constant uncertainty that made me push you away.

That night at the bar, I walked over to straddle your lap, driving my soaking crotch against yours. You buried your face in my barely covered breasts and your fingers explored the garters under my skirt. But I knew you still wanted her, even after we went back to your place and made love in the backyard under the stars and your neighbors' lit windows.

Love? I'm not sure I should call it that. If I do I might not recognize it when I have it for real. Lust, obsession: They come closer. Still, it was more than that. Once when I was sick, you brought me chicken soup and old videos. We sat and watched Dietrich in *Morocco* and, of course, Garbo in everything.

That was almost like love, wasn't it? Except for all those times you weren't there and I had to wonder if you were bringing chicken soup to someone else. I couldn't bear to go back to La Strada after we went there, you know. I quit my job so I wouldn't see Mark again. I haven't worn the leather skirt since our last night together. You don't know how often I've wished that you ignored the fight I picked with you then, that you had fixed me with the look that made me melt and let me bury my face in your shoulder and forget what I knew. It would have at least prolonged the inevitable.

But tonight, tonight I hold the memories at arm's length and survey them critically. Are they enough to fill tomorrow night and the night after? My free hand strokes the inside of my thigh and I try to imagine that it's yours. Even this gentle pleasure brings only a shadow of what we once had. Perhaps remembering will not be enough. Still, I run quickly through some of the good memories as though they were in a card file.

You sent me chocolate-covered strawberries at work the only Valentine's Day that we were together. I check the dates in my journal in disbelief. Six months? Only six months of last year to leave your

5

fingerprints inside me, indelible marks of time spent with you. Perhaps I am too sensitive. Perhaps I should be over you by now. Perhaps I will be. Now. Tonight.

I remember your smile whenever you saw me. I remember the readings we went to, the music we heard, the talks we had. The way you held my hand when we walked down the street. Not all the time, but enough to make it count. Thank you for that.

Thank you, too, for this. Tonight I will put aside my pen and I will put on my armor, my black leather skirt and my fishnets, my red lace bra and my leather bustier. I will slip one of these little metal balls inside me until I run molten and my nipples harden into permanent points.

Then I will gather my friends together and I will go first to La Strada and then to one of your clubs. And when I see you there, I'll be sure to fuck someone else.

THE FOURTEENTH DAY

Experts estimate that ovulation occurs on the fourteenth day of a woman's menstrual cycle—approximately two weeks after she starts one period, and two weeks before the next. Around the time the egg is released, the secretions in the vagina change, the breasts and abdomen swell slightly, and sometimes there is even mid-month cramping. Thus, a woman's journey to the red sea begins.

For some women, the fourteenth day is simply the beginning of bloating and irritability, but for me it is all that and more. It is the dawn of intense horniness. So what if my pants don't fit for two weeks afterward? I remind myself that my swollen stomach also means a nice, slick, swollen pussy covered in nerve endings that tell me it's time to fuck and fuck, and then fuck once again for good measure.

Unfortunately, all that unmonitored fucking can lead to myriad dilemmas, one of which is unwanted pregnancy. I had (inadvertently) circumvented that situation with lesbianism. Of course, I was raised to be a good heterosexual girl who would one day marry and reproduce, but when I got out of college, my life took a nontraditional turn. I discovered women. Luscious, passionate goddesses. Some were fleshy and feminine; others, wiry and masculine. And then there were all the variations thereof: robust stone butches, androdykes, delicate girly girls, outrageous lipstick divas, married bisexuals, the list goes on. During these experimentations, I came across a butch dyke, Shannon, who could push all my buttons. She loved to play games, and after four years together, could tune in to my hormonal cycle down to its slightest tick.

With Shannon and all the women before her, I was free to enjoy my fourteenth day without the worry of the nitty-gritty of male/female, sperm/egg amalgamations. My world revolved around lusty romps in the hay and adoration of my ever-swelling female territories, some of which I had only previously read about in textbooks. Best of all, Shannon rarely said no to sex, no matter how many times we had already fucked. Sometimes even I couldn't keep up with her—but on the fourteenth day, she had to keep up with me instead.

"Are you horny again?" Shannon asked me one afternoon and gave me a pinch on the nipple. "Was twice not enough?"

I looked down at my larger-than-usual breasts rolling off the sides of my chest, my pudgy stomach and my hand that stroked my lips with increasing determination.

"Yeah, sure it was enough, baby. I'm worn out," I reassured her. I pulled my eager hand away from my pussy and tugged on the bristly hairs of her fresh crewcut to draw her down for a kiss. But my fingers slipped through the stubble and landed back on my tummy. *Fat tummy. Damn. I was skinnier yesterday. What's up with this?* Seemingly overnight, I had morphed into a fertility goddess figurine. I pulled the sheet back up to my tits, not to conceal my cuntplay so much as to hide my increasing puffiness.

Once I was covered, I moved my hand down my taut, round belly toward the wetness again. Hidden, my body still seemed distorted, yet beautiful. But the bloat is the first sign of readiness, I reminded myself. So let the games begin!

Shannon had resumed her Sunday morning TV marathon, spent strap-on at her side. I peeked over at her strong thighs, her knee with the old skateboarding scar, the downy layer of hair on her lower shins, her clean, unpainted toenails. Before I knew it, I had my fingers back inside my pussy, still creamy from her lips and cock. The bed began to squeak as it had just twenty minutes before when I'd had her full attention. Part of me hoped she wouldn't hear over the blaring racecars on TV. Another part of me bounced even louder and harder to make her look.

"What is up with you today?" she asked.

"I don't know, baby," I murmured. "I just feel so crazy." By that time I had my middle finger deep inside my cunt, the knuckles tightly lodged inside the ribbed shaft and the fingertip throbbing against my G spot.

"Can we?" I panted, sitting up to look her in the eye. "Can we play that game again? It's time. Please?"

She knew the game, of course. We played it every month. I called it "The Fourteenth Day." In it, the boy fucks his girlfriend and gets her pregnant against her will. After half a life of menstruation, I had come to know the exact day and hour that I released my egg. Each time, I was left with a tingly feeling of anticipation, as if something very special had happened. I was wide open, somehow ready to take on the world— fertile, engorged, inflated, and teetering on the verge of fireworks.

My butch inched her harness back up over her hips, threw me down on the pillows and bound me with the strength of her sinewy chest, her slender ass in the air, denying me thick penetration.

"OK, so tell me, what exactly does my little girl want now?"

I wiggled around under her flattened breasts. "I . . . I want you to fuck me."

She pressed harder and glared at me. "But do you know what you're getting yourself into? You're playing with fire, sweetie."

"I don't know about all that," I lied. "I just want to feel good, and it does feel so good . . . my finger is so big inside me already, I can hardly stand it." I hunched my pelvis up toward the dildo so that it slid across my parted wet lips and knuckles. So close. Unprotected.

"Well, you know I can fill you up even better than that measly finger. And you're ripe for the pickin'." She jerked my fingers out of my cunt, so I rested them nonchalantly on my clit.

"But you can't do this to me!" I squealed. "Not like this! I'm not on the Pill!"

"I don't care," she said, as she widened my opening with her cock. "I'll do whatever I want. You know my balls are tight and full of come. You go teasin' me like that and you'll pay, little girl." With those words, she shoved the rest of the cock inside of me. I swooned, my nervous little hand sandwiched between our pubic hair.

"Please stop! Put a condom on! You have to!"

"Don't tell me what to do." She began to thrust. I rubbed my clit to the rhythm. "I'm going to come inside of you and take that egg," she said. "It's mine now." It was a tight fit from the fourteenth day swelling. I felt every inch of her. Although we used the same dildo as earlier, it seemed to have doubled in girth. "Yep, I'm gonna come. I'm gonna shoot this sperm right up inside you."

"No! Stop! We can't!" I protested, and pulled her even closer. Her back was strong and broad, yet tapered into a womanly waist. She had a devilish gleam in her eyes; my butch loved to play the big bad wolf.

"Ha ha, too late, my pretty. You're gonna have my baby! You just wait!"

With that, I worked my clit into a frenzy, clenched down on her cock, and drained it as I came. She filled me up with her ejaculation, covered my internal girly organs with the most dangerous solution known to woman—semen. Semen on the fourteenth day to boot. There was no escape. Sperm plus egg . . . oh no! What had I done? My life was ruined. Mother Nature had duped me. I lost my breath for a moment.

But ah, my butch's cock was sterile and safe. No babies, no nonsense, no fuss. *We* had duped Mother Nature.

Shannon and I stayed together for another year or so, but eventually "just friends" became our watchword. It took a year to get over the relationship and all the kinky games we had created. I decided not to have sex with anyone for a while, so I slipped away from my lesbian circles to reduce the temptation. I hung out with artistic crowds, eccentrics of both genders. Soon I found myself flirting again, even with boys, straight and gay. I needed to play.

After the long dating drought and some reconsideration of the male animal, I took on a handsome lover, a gentle jazz pianist named Jim—a boy born with a penis, so different from the many cocks and boys I'd known who had not been born together. It had been a decade since I had slept with a man, and I'd truly had no intention of ever getting so close to real live sperm again. But for some reason, I felt especially comfortable with this unassuming, courteous creature, so I said yes to heterosexuality once more.

Sex with a man was intriguing, yet unsettling. As I removed Jim's condom one night, my finger encountered a drop of semen, the very juice that had coursed through my former fantasies. It was warm, and gooey like the conditioner I used on my hair. The thick fluid was a bit repulsive, but it was his and I loved him and every ounce of his body. I inspected it in the dim light.

"What are you doing?" he asked.

"Nothing. I'm just looking at how good I made you come," I answered. "There must be five ounces in here." My womb stirred again.

I kissed him and dangled the sack above his stomach. Suddenly I remembered this was the real deal: it was nocuous white cream full of tiny squirming larvae, waiting to plague my life. It reeked of mushrooms, squealing pigs, flesh and blood tornados, green aliens, broken lightbulbs, and eighteen years minimum emotional and financial obligation. Fantasy is one thing, but reality is . . . reality. I jumped off the bed and ran into the bathroom. In no time, the used condom was in the trash and my hands had undergone obsessive-compulsive scrubbing.

My fourteenth day came and went every month, and I made sure to milk my time dry—but with careful latex barriers. And then one day I decided to share my whimsy.

"That feels so good," Jim sighed. I took my mouth off his cock and toyed with his balls in deep contemplation.

"You know what, honey?"

"What?" He was on the brink of orgasm and probably didn't care to hear me talk. He guided my head back to his cock. "Please don't stop

11

now." I could tell he needed to come, and soon, but I stopped anyway. He'd get to come soon enough.

"With these nice balls, I bet you could get me pregnant in a heartbeat." I kissed the head of his cock playfully.

Jim froze. "Don't scare me like that!"

"No, what I mean is that you probably could get me pregnant if you wanted to, but you won't. Let's just play a game and pretend instead." I got on my hands and knees and stuck my ass in the air. He knew what I wanted—doggie style, deep and thorough. My fingers scrambled around on the bedside table to find my trusty vibrator and a condom for him. Jim hesitated a bit, but couldn't resist playing once I started rubbing my ass cheeks against his hard cock. He put the condom on with finesse.

"Don't you realize what a little animal I am?" I hinted. "I just ovulated and I'm extra horny." I turned on the vibrator and pressed it above my clit. "And you're just a big beast." Visions of does and wild bucks scampered across my brain. "I think you were put here on this planet to fuck me."

And he did, as hard as he could.

"And you're here to take it," he added.

I came in waves, not once, but twice (as I tend to do with the vibrator). The walls of my cunt shivered, pulled, and squeezed until I finally felt him jerk three times inside of me. With a piggish grunt, he filled me with that mysterious fuel male beings store in their tanks. It sent me speeding into a tragic world where nature takes its course regardless of what is right or wrong. We'd fucked with abandon, driven by desires much stronger than love. We had, like all the other creatures, submitted to Mother Nature on that fateful fourteenth day.

Fortunately, Jim and I, evolved beings that we are, had taken precautions against Mother Nature's cunning scheme. Unfortunately, you can't fool her all the time. Sometimes she tries to get revenge.

Jim's cock softened, and the full condom wriggled between his flesh and mine. I panicked once again. He was no butch with a silicone dildo. He was a real man with real sperm who could really impregnate me. I was way too fertile and the condom was starting to slip. I lay down flat on my stomach to escape. Or was it already too late? Once unlinked, we bolted from the bed to the bathroom and spent our post-coital cuddling time apart. I stood in the bathtub washing my pussy with the showerhead. Jim cleaned his cock in the sink. Hardly romantic.

Amid the suds and cold porcelain, I explained my monthly visions. Soon the fantasy talk turned into a discussion of real-life reproductive goals (or lack thereof), plans for the future, marriage, debt, careers. Another mood-killer. From that day on, I was unable to relax on my fourteenth day.

Shortly thereafter, I went to the gynecologist and got on the Pill. There were no more messy condoms or risk of accidents, and no more water retention, but my precious fourteenth day quit arriving. The new hormones stretched and flattened my cycle into a series of monochromatic days. I didn't complain to Jim or the doctor. The consequences of not taking the Pill were too severe.

Yet I missed our fourteenth day celebration, the Easter egg hunt, the ebb and flow, the waxing and waning of my tummy. Most of all, I missed my fertility. No matter how I might use it in my lifetime, it still had been mine to flaunt.

As luck would have it, nature intervened once again: The extra estrogen gave me high blood pressure, so I leapt off the Pill without regret. We considered other methods of birth control, but Jim opted for the ultimate. The vasectomy. The perfect solution.

Today Jim's balls have long since healed and life is good. We are thrilled with the freedom. Now that I'm off the Pill, my fourteenth day arrives every month again, breast tenderness, balloon-gut and all. I pounce on Jim as soon as I feel the tug in my womb, eager to play perverted baby-making games with his newly sterilized cock and balls. However, the fun always starts in the same awkward way:

"Honey, guess what? I'm fertile again. It's time for you to . . . " I run my hand down the skin that covers my biological clock.

"Wait," he says nervously. "Now, are you wanting a baby or something? After all this?"

"No, I swear. Don't you remember?"

"But you keep talking about it."

"I like to pretend. You must know how I am by now."

"Are you sure that's all? Because I really didn't want kids, but I would have done it for you. It's too late now, but we could adopt later if you just had to have one, or I could try to get a reversal. I hope I didn't . . . "

"Hush, now. This is perfect." I sit up and take his cock in my hand. "Just get me pregnant, but leave the baby out of it."

He lets out a perturbed sigh and turns his back to me. My request always seems to startle him for a bit. Then he reels back around and tears open my thighs.

"Pregnant, you say? With no baby? In your dreams!" With that, he slams me down on the bed and impales me with all his force. His cock feels gargantuan inside my puffed-up pussy. As much as I want him, I squeal and fight, pounding his chest and trying to close my legs. Jim bites my ear and growls, "I lied. There was no vasectomy! You've been lucky so far, but you just wait. I'll get you yet!"

Sterilized risk. On the fourteenth day.

CAGES

E very day, I feel you looking at me as I walk by you on the street. Don't think I don't. Your eyes practically leave prints on my ass, as if they were grubby little fingers. And don't you wish they were? You may be thinking, "Look at her eyebrows, she's a real redhead—I wonder if her juicy little pussy has freckles and red hair too?" or even, "What a bitch, she won't even look me in the eye."

Oh yes, I can hear those sorts of thoughts. And you're right about me. On both counts.

When I say "you" I mean all of you, all of you who love women. A billion eyes staring, all with something in common. I've known you for a long time. When you look at me now, it reminds me of something that happened when I was very young, when I was first learning how to deal with you, learning how to meet your gaze. These days, you don't look at me quite the same way. Not because I've changed physically; I've been this tall ever since I was fifteen, and have always worn my hair this long. I'm sure I could still fit into my Catholic school uniform. My face has grown up somewhat, but that's not what has changed. You don't look at me the same way now because I'm often the one looking at you, with thoughts that make most of you cower. And you feel it.

But that's now. To tell the story that's in my memory, I'll go back to when I was just out of high school.

When I was that young, I wouldn't look at you when I was out on the street. It wasn't because I wouldn't have liked to fuck you. I probably would have. But of course you don't invite every woman who passes you on the street into your bed. And I can't fuck you all anyhow. But if you were to have come to see me at the job I had back then I'd have looked at you, all right, when I was safely behind glass with the other girls. Where I return, at least in my head, in order to tell you my story.

It isn't really a job to me. I don't need the money. I usually work once a week, on Sundays, or when I skip a dance class. Yes, I'm just what I look like to you from where you stand in your booth behind the glass or one-way mirror: a snotty ballerina with rich parents forever away at their summer house. And I'm good, too. On my way to the City Ballet. This place is my dirty little secret. And yours, too. All of you out there in the dark. The pathetic ones who can't keep their noses wiped, the lonely ones, the frightened, the angry, and the curious.

I like to watch the lonely ones best. I understand why you're here: It's comforting as well as arousing to look at women. Women embody the coziness and delighted fulfillment you wish you could recapture now that you're out in the cold, out of the womb. They're made to be looked at, and so you do. You look. I do it myself, here, or at home in my room in my family's big empty house: I steal my brother's magazines, strip naked except for high heels and one of my grandmother's mink coats, worn fur-side in. I stretch out on the floor next to a mirror. Sometimes I touch myself while I look at the pictures, but mostly I just cuddle into the fur. I feel beautiful then, realizing I'm one of them, one of the goddesses. I like to look at the pictures of blondes, the ones with the honey-colored halos of fleece on pussies with complicated, fantastic lips like orchid petals, cunts that look like they've been warmed by the sun and glow golden from the inside.

I could tell you about the other girls here in this mirrored cage with me. They don't all see the depth of their own beauty, and most treat themselves with contempt. Some of these girls think they're worth nothing more than this, but this belief isn't usually something that you out there with your eyes full of desire would ever notice. They don't think this on the surface: It's underneath their conscious thought. It's easy to tell yourself you're valuable even while you're a whore, even if you're one of the ones who gets drunk or high every night just to come here and dance. Or to come here and watch, for that matter. Think about it. Maybe you do it to yourself. Maybe you believe you're strong, a success, when really you're fucking yourself over in a hundred ways every day, whoring yourself in an empty life because you think it's what you should do.

For instance, you, the lonely ones. You don't have women in your lives and think you can't find one in the outside world. Or maybe you do have women, ones who don't do everything in bed that you wish they would. So you come here. You turn to strangers to get a taste of what you want, what you think you can't have. You bring your straining erections with you, held protectively in your laps like small dogs you're taking to the vet.

Some days I'm bored and could care less, but sometimes I want to look at you, imagine you. I'm not supposed to touch myself in front of the customers, but maybe I will, for you. Just a little. My fingers will do reconnaissance for your desire. You all keep putting coins in. Some of you look at me in a way I like. But don't expect anything from me. This only works if I think you don't expect anything from me except a dose of beauty, and the chance to look as long as you like without being made to feel like a criminal. This is the place, if you're respectful and you happen to sit where I can see you when the door comes up. In the corner booths, the ones with shaded windows. You and I form a temporary closed circuit here, with you looking at me like that. When I feel that the beauty has run out of me, your gaze tells me it hasn't. I look at the other girls here and see they all have their admirers, too: even the flat, the short, the fat, the scrawny. Men are far less critical of women than women are.

No, I'm not saying women are nothing without you who admire us. But what are we without each other? I didn't always feel this way. For years I thought I should feel fear, shame, or anger when you looked at me. I thought it meant I was an object for you to use. But of course it's not that simple; power never sits on just one side of an equation.

You're wondering what it would feel like to touch me. Yes, they're sensitive, my nipples. They stand up just because your eyes are resting on them. They're a dusky pink that someday will fade. I'll wear rouge on them when that happens. But I'll bet my freckles won't fade. You'd like to count them all with your tongue, wouldn't you? I can imagine you doing it. My breasts are small, but they're real. Delicate enough to really feel your mouth and hands on them, with a tragically vulnerable feminine shape. A real shape: an architecture that swoops and curves for the eye, a structure that sits heavy and dense in the hand.

The rest of the inventory: "Hey, Red, those legs look good all the way up. Love that short skirt." I've heard that before. And my ass is magnificent, as you can see. It's the only bountiful stop on this long ride. Sometimes I swing it even more lasciviously when I walk past you on the street, feeling your hot little optical fingerprints on it. Because nestled between my hipbones and hidden beyond my ass is the red-hot coal of my cunt. My center, my creative mind. At these times, I'm imagining what I'd like to do to you—or have you do to me. Those thoughts of doing and being done unto depend on my mood. Sometimes I'm a bitch goddess of pain who wants to tease you and hear you beg, and sometimes I'm a whore. Ah, whore. That word again.

Right about now you may be wondering when I'll stop teasing and tell you my story. It's not teasing. It's a privileged glimpse into my thoughts. Here's a tip for you: The key is to be patient enough to stay in control of yourself while still keeping in mind what you want.

I wonder, if you were allowed to touch me, would you really know how to enjoy me? Would you appreciate the sunken bead necklace of my spine, the wings of my shoulder blades? Would you notice the miracle of my belly, its slight raised oval in the middle and concavity at the hipbones and ribs? Would you figure out that your tongue could fit in my navel like a foot in a slipper? How I'd arch up against you if you put your mouth on me just right?

18

Would you worship my pussy for the amazing thing that it is: hungrier than a lioness, deep as the ocean? I'll tell you how to approach it correctly, to wallow and suffer in its treasure and appease its cruelty. Because it is cruel, as cruel as your cock can be, maybe more so. It mocks, it deflates, but only out of a need to protect itself. It's like the vulnerable octopus: It must be crafty to survive. Maybe you think I'm being coy with my description. But you should know this trap of pleasure between women's thighs can be as much a mystery to us as it is to you. I don't envy you one bit, having to decipher it. But I can tell you one thing: Don't underestimate its strength, should you become its prey.

A pussy, you see, is a queendom of many parts. As a queendom, it works like this: Each part demands recognition and tribute. It's best if you start at the hinterlands and slowly approach the castle, with its treasury and throne room, by the main road. At least the first time. Once you know the queen, all the rules change. She often has a heart of butter. But not when it comes to spear-shaking barbarian hordes at her gates.

Once you know she's yours (or you're hers), and you've made it past the eyes, mouth, hands, arms, feet, legs and everything else, start at the belly or inner thighs. I don't care how you do it, just make a stop of some kind. A word, a caress, a taste. The curls are next: breathe on them, brush them with your lips, stroke them. Admire. The outside of the outer lips come next, and the seam where they meet (if they do meet; some cunts are like pansies, with pouty outer lips that conceal small, vivid centers; and some are like fuchsias, all rococo frills and dangles of interior complexity).

No, don't hurry. There's time. You should know the inside of the outer lips is a different country from the planes of the inner lips, and from the clitoris, and from the circuitous folds all around. Now you're starting to understand, aren't you? A tiny world, but very detailed. Remember the miracle of your own tongue, of your fingers, your lips, your teeth. The tip of the tongue is different from the flat of it, sucking is distinct from biting, circular licks are for teasing, tasting. And when it comes to rhythm or stroke, I shouldn't have to tell you anything, should I?

19

Keep going from there, after lengthy stops at each oasis. The velvet sleeve inside is all about fingers, tongues, angles, positions, compatibilities. The combinations change kaleidoscopically with each pairing of lovers, so you're on your own now. I won't insult your intelligence with more specifics. You're engineers. You're laborers. You're connoisseurs. Follow your noses, your eyes, your taste buds, your pricks.

Ah, yes, back to your pricks. I can still see them out there in the dark. You like how I'm moving now, don't you? This is the language of motion, sweat and foreplay. This is trance and meditation. This is what I do alone in my room when there's no one and nothing to satisfy the ache. These ripples and undulations and unwavering gazes are all fed by inner heat. I am more naked than naked here, with your mirrored eyes drinking in my body. Some of you like it if I crawl away from you, looking over my shoulder, wearing the haughty expression of a princess bitch. You like the come-hither/go-away dichotomy, the I'm-yours/forget-it conundrum. I can't move this way in ballet, of course. But that's why I love ballet, the repression of it—every impulse and desire must be fit into a form cruel to the human body. There is freedom in the constant struggle against strength, time, and physics. Ballet as an art form is dead without passion striving to escape from it.

And maybe you're thinking I'm a bit young to know all this. Where did I pick it up? Some of it I've learned through dreaming, hours spent by myself. And reading. God love books for what they can teach you, here and there.

Oh, you out there in the seats, watching. You want me to go back to talking about your pricks again? Or at least, you say, give you more details about me and my pussy. No. You don't really need details. You can make up any story you like about me. It's what you're here for, isn't it? You want to be fooled, to be indulged. To project your desires and fantasies while I'm dancing here under the lights. All this in the guise of being entertained. It's an endless tease. You must like the torment. And maybe I do too.

I'll admit: I've never seen anyone out there watching whom I wanted in a serious way. This isn't about falling in love, after all. This is about lust and fucking. Sometimes there's nothing like an anonymous face, cock, or pair of hands for that. Someone I don't ever want to see again. Someone who represents the universal male principle for an hour, a great faceless erection, someone to play god to my goddess. Someone I even look down on, despise a little, because he's chasing everything he thinks he's missed in life by sniffing after me in his middle years, begging for a taste.

I used to work in a different kind of place, one with stages and couches and tables, endlessly hustling the customers to buy me drinks so the house would make its money. Dancing at the customers' tables. That was more dangerous than this, to be that close to you all, with your bristly faces, your hands and clothes stained with motor oil or mass-produced cologne, your breath smelling of cigarettes, alcohol, peppermint, longing, anger.

At first I used to keep reminding you customers not to touch me, but your hands were relentless, unceasing. If I got tired, all I had to do was push my breasts in your faces and you'd be happy to sit like that for the entire song, most of you, hoping my thigh would brush up against your crotch as I pretended to dance. Onstage, I was everything and everyone. With the red lights shining in my eyes, I couldn't see you, but I knew you were there. On the floor, I always wore long gloves, clouds of perfume, a bored look on my face. That way none of you ever knew what I was thinking or could really touch me. The really determined among you would come in with a plan: to have me meet you later for lunch, for a drink, for breakfast. Promises of money, modeling jobs, dinners in elegant hotels, of being made into a kept woman. Or just a request to flash you, let you slip your fingers inside my costume, for twice the price of a regular dance.

And did I ever? Let's say I did. Let's say I was capable of being worn down by constant visits from one of you, by his pleadings, compliments, guilt trips. By his pathetic need that wasn't as helpless as it seemed, and the fact that he and I both knew it.

Maybe it flattered or amused me. Maybe his life was just so alien from

21

mine that I took the tour he offered. Let's say I did meet him once for lunch at a hotel downtown, listened to his speeches, was persuaded by the hundred-dollar bill he always gave me at the club just so that I'd sit and talk with him and then dance for one song. Was I surprised when he mentioned during lunch that he'd rented a room upstairs? Did I need the money he slid across the table under a napkin?

What do you think?

If there was a man like this, he was effectively all of you at once. Nameless. So I will address him as "you," as in: I remember you had a favorite costume you liked me to wear at the club, a white one with rhinestones and fringe. As in: You liked to riffle the edges of the white fringe with your finger, liked the pillowed shelf the top made out of my breasts. As in: It wasn't really me that you wanted, Mr. Customer. You wanted a particular pussy you'd chosen and carefully groomed to trust you this far. One with my type of face, my length of legs, my color hair. You knew the value, the price per pound, of this flavor of youth and beauty, and thought you had a plan that would allow you to enjoy it.

You smelled so nervous as we stood in the elevator after lunch. You watched me in the orange-tinted mirrors and probably thought I'd never looked so bored. You were sure I despised you, your ordinary face and ordinary life, no longer young, but you couldn't let yourself shine a light on those thoughts for even an instant. You trembled before me, the young cunt you thought you'd fooled, you'd bought, you'd won over with your persistence, with almost a year's worth of visits at the club. And I thought I'd fooled you. I'd call you by your name, but I doubt you gave me your real one. I certainly didn't give you mine. I was your magic, your disposable miracle, and that's what I wanted to be.

I gambled that you weren't dangerous. No, I could see you weren't. Not with the way you showed me your room, the way you had a bottle of vodka already out on the dresser. The way the bed was perfectly square and smooth in its floral spread. You took my coat from my shoulders, and your touch made me recoil, made me shiver. Made me so wet that with every step I felt as if I were sliding, as if I could soak through my clothes. You might as well have been a drooling, dirty pervert, with cracked, leathery hands rough enough to snag on my skin. That's the part you played. You didn't try to hide your lust, though you were practical enough to have brought condoms. You didn't know what to do at first when I didn't want the drink you offered. You sat on the edge of the bed and asked me to come to you, and your voice was dry, brittle. Maybe you were worried that you wouldn't be able to get it up, that I'd laugh at you and your paunch and receding hair, your poorly trimmed beard. If you were, you didn't let it show at the time. You looked as though you felt tall, in control. Here I was in your room, and I came over when you asked me to. You saw that you were finally going to be able to do it, to put your big square hands on me. That I was finally going to let you fuck me.

I know now, if I didn't know then, that you were afraid, because you got up and went to sit in a chair, asked me to strip for you. Just like at the club. The familiar thing. Some song on the radio, your breath fogging my cleavage, you murmuring under your breath, "Oh yeah, oh yes." Me stripped down to my underwear, my thigh rubbing against your hard-on. Your hands touching me, taking off my bra.

I must have felt very soft and smooth to you when you lifted my tits and squeezed them a little, your fingers pinching the nipples. All the while you looked at them, mesmerized. Your lips were thin, dry. All you could think to do was suckle on me, your hands interrupting to squeeze both breasts a few more times. Your breathing was loud, rasping my ears. You were practically shaking, bound up in electricity. "Oh God," you whispered. "Show me. Show me your pussy. Spread it open." But not there, not right close to you. You wanted me on my back on the bed, my legs apart. So you could watch from where you were. First, just to tease you, I pulled my G-string aside, one leg bent and the other flat against the bedspread. Just a flash, a glimpse. You unzipped your fly and freed your cock while you watched me. "Take off those panties," you said. "Touch it. Move your hips around."

I put my fingers in my mouth, moved them in and out, sent them down wet to pinch my nipples. I was slow to finally lift my hips and peel my underwear off for you, to part my auburn nest and show you the gleaming depths, the tiny hooded erection in the center. That's all it took to get you out of your chair. Your beard tickled the insides of my thighs as you knelt to lick me, your fingers tugging my lips apart. I saw the top of your head with its combed-over strands of hair bobbing up and down, and I was reminded of a dog lapping ice cream off the sidewalk. There was no queendom in this, like I described before, no finesse, but none was needed: This was an electrified fuck, never meant to be, and never to be repeated. Neither of us cared, or needed, to win the other over. Your tongue stabbed at my cunt; my clit was on fire. You may have been deliberately clumsy, reaching up and squeezing my breasts harder now, rhythmic as a chant or a demand for salvation, as your tongue burrowed into me. You went down on me to keep me away, because your fear had come back—of the uncertainty of it all, of who was running this. And I was glad of it.

The folded money, wrapped in a napkin, burned and glowed where I'd tucked it away on my purse, sitting on the dresser. I couldn't see it, but I could feel it. My cunt throbbed with so much heat it blinded me to everything but shame and danger and power. All my life I'd been raised as something precious, too valuable for the likes of you, and here I was trading the priceless ruby between my legs to a lecherous goat for money. It was my choice.

I slid off the bed and bent myself over the couch, ass in the air and feet on the floor. You didn't wait to be invited. Your hairy legs were there against me, your hands on me. As you put the condom on you realized we were reflected in the mirrors on the closet doors, and you watched yourself. Watched as you held your prick, guided it, sank it into me. Pressed me hard against the back of the couch, one hand on either side of my ass, your fingers digging in, lifting me. You closed your eyes for a moment when you were in me all the way, and called on Jesus. At first you moved slowly, watching the shining length of your cock slide out and then all the way back in, over and over again. As if seeing this confirmed the reality of its happening, of your control over it. And then it was just your ass moving, humping faster and faster, a wordless groan coming out of your mouth until you grew more coherent, whispering, "I'm fucking you, I'm fucking you," like a plea for mercy. I wasn't watching any more, by that point. I was coming like a string of fire-crackers going off, one after another, the salty cloth of the upholstery between my teeth, and I didn't care about you. We were even.

Afterward, when your spent and shriveled cock slipped out of me, I felt that coiling slither in my belly: shame. This was sin. I thought I was ruined, used and defiled by you. I had felt what I thought was utter helplessness, and utter power. I had never been so alive, or so in pain. It had all been my decision.

On the outside, I appeared cool as ever. Or if I didn't, you weren't in a state to notice. I dressed and left with the money, without replying to anything you said. Despising you felt good then. The next time I got drunk, I thought back over it, over you, and was immediately sick. Later, I used the money you gave me to buy a Christmas present for my mother, a piece of antique silver for her collection. You never came back to the club to see me again—or maybe it was that I quit working there soon after, to go dance in a mirrored cage instead.

What do I think of all this now? That guilt and shame over consensual sex are useless, enervating. I prefer the wisdom of the body. It never lies, when you ask it directly. If what happened that night had been so very wrong, where did the electricity come from, the taste of primal forces? It was an equitable transaction, even one in which I came out ahead. It was my initiation into risk, danger, power, into living by my own laws. I wanted to be desired by someone who understood I was worth the trouble. It sounds cold, but that was how my life worked then. My few other lovers up until that time had been forbidden fruit as well, but not like this was.

These days I still deal with passion striving against its bonds. Not just in dance, but with the bodies of the men who pay handsomely to see me. They come to feel the pain and restriction I give them, the beautiful cruelty. Just like when I was stripping for them. The rule is still "no touching," and now I am the one who enforces it as I please.

You could, I suppose, apply the term "whore" to me now. But my clients, bound and blindfolded and touched by my lash, will never utter that word in my presence, nor would it cross their minds to use it except to apply it to themselves.

What delicious confusion there is in these traps of words and power and passion, guilt and choices and glass booths with coin-operated windows, all these fantastical, baroque cages. I am mistress over them now, both the literal and the figurative ones. I've caught many a rare creature in them, some for love and some for money. And I live a life I've created for myself, the life I want. I'm the ballerina with an enigmatic smile.

So when you see me, a real redhead with tresses sculpted in a sleek knot, all long limbs confined by proper form and a carefully schooled expression, go ahead and wink. But be warned: Sometimes I wink back.

I couldn't think straight. I hardly even noticed when the water turned cold as I stood in the shower, imagining my new man's hands on my body. They were strong hands, thin, with long fingers, palms calloused from years of wheelchair use. I wanted to feel that roughness against my skin, the power of those long, lean arms pushing me, pulling me, overwhelming me.

It wasn't until I began to shiver that I finally made my way out of the shower and back into my room. The simple act of getting dressed seemed to take up three times the time it normally did, and I caught myself, not once but twice, standing half-dressed and dreamy-eyed, the process of getting ready for work quite forgotten. I was doomed to lateness, protested the sensible, good-worker part of me, and yet I could not bring myself to care. I could still see his easy smile, hear him laughing even at the worst of my puns. My cheeks still hurt from grinning at his.

And to think I'd almost passed up the chance to meet him at all.

"Hey, Kristen," Jane had said to me, "How long has it been since you and Kyle called it quits?"

"A year and a half," I replied, my tone somewhat guarded.

"Exactly. Don't you just want to get out for a little while?"

"Not particularly, why?" I responded.

"Well, honey, I know you have work and all, but, really, doesn't it get a little dull?"

"I'm not really interested in the whole dating scene right now, Jane. I just haven't got time for it, let alone energy."

"Oh, come on! You need to get out once in a while, Kris. You'll go nuts without at least a little fun in your life. Don't tell me you aren't dying for an excuse to get out of the apartment."

"What is this all about, anyway?" I asked quietly.

"Oh, you know, I just know someone—a friend from college. He'd be really great for you, I think."

"I'm really not interested right now, Jane," I said more firmly. "Not at all. Maybe sometime, but not right now. Thanks for the offer, though, really."

"I think you'd really like him, though. I imagine you'd have a lot in common."

"Oh?" I replied, but my voice said "prove it."

"Yeah, you know. Well, he's in a wheelchair. He has a disability."

"Really? Wow! Does he have eyes, too? We're practically twins!" I replied, teasingly. Why it is that able-bodied people always assume all us crips are automatically made for each other, I will never know.

"Okay, point taken," Jane said, mildly abashed. "But that's not the only reason I like the idea of you two together," she added quickly as she noticed me preparing to get to my feet, cane in my left hand. "He's a great guy. Really."

"I'll think about it." My voice betrayed my lingering reluctance as I got up.

"Oh, wait, wait!" she exclaimed, bolting out of her seat on the couch. "Wait a second."

I waited. She emerged from her bedroom a few moments later, depositing a snapshot in my hand. In it, she knelt beside a beaming green-eyed, sandy-haired man—my would-be date. I hadn't meant to even really look at the picture until I returned to my apartment on the ground floor of the building, but something about his eyes caught me as I glanced down into my palm. I knew then that I could get lost in those eyes, that I wanted to. Maybe I already was. I wanted him to smile the way he smiled in that photo for me. Because of me. I wanted, to my sudden shock, to see that sandy wave of hair drip dark with sweat, to see what his face looked like in ecsta—

"Well?" she asked, then, grinning.

"I'll think about it," I said quietly, hoping my cheeks weren't as red as they felt.

"You'll go out with him. Just dinner."

"Yeah, okay. Dinner. I'll . . . yeah."

Snapping out of my quiet reverie, I blinked several times before my gaze shot down to my wrist. Nearly an hour late. Shit, shit, shit. Pausing only long enough to grab my cane from its usual spot in the umbrella stand, I hurried to work, leaving my lunch sitting in a small brown bag on the kitchen counter.

I should've stayed home. I much preferred vague and distant feelings of goldbricker's guilt to endless pointless hours staring blankly at my unchanging computer screen in full view of my boss and coworkers. But there were always stupid idle tasks, things that could be done while I listened to the news on the radio and thought of Michael and the dinner we'd shared the night before. And grinned like an idiot.

God, he was amazing. I had to talk to him again. Everything else seemed so damn dull around the edges. I stared at the phone. I had told him I would call. And I would. It would certainly be one of the most productive things I could do in my current, dazed, state. I considered for a moment the potential reactions of my boss and coworkers if they were to walk past my door and catch me wasting yet more time murmuring dreamily into my phone to Michael, but I couldn't really bring myself to care. One phone call wouldn't change the overall trajectory of my day here at work one iota. I had to tame the butterflies in my stomach, that was all. In the end, I managed to waste a lot of time on the phone calling everyone but Michael. Jane was particularly happy with the report I gave her, and then she went on about this and that with her characteristic enthusiasm, babbling at length while I thought of Michael's eyes, his hands. Finally Jane fell silent. To my embarrassment, I entirely failed to notice.

"You're thinking about him, aren't you?" Jane teased when I finally sputtered an apology for being so out to lunch. "For God's sake, Kris, *call him*. Are you going to call him?"

"Sure," I said without thinking.

"Good. Then I'll let you get to it," my friend said, and hung up.

Before I realized what I was doing I was halfway through a breathless monologue: " . . . so refreshing to finally meet someone with a sense of humor so similar to mine. I think we really need to start taking advantage of this. I'm completely without anything to do tonight, and, well, I was thinking of renting some comedies or something, you know? Would you want to come over and watch them with me? I mean, sometime? I know you're probably busy."

"Yes," he replied, the grin audible in his voice. "That would be really great."

"Really?" I replied stupidly.

"Really," he affirmed. "Definitely. Tonight is great."

"Well, let's see." I thought of my apartment, mentally calculating how much time I'd need to make it look like a seductive love nest, or at least a hell of a lot less like your average war zone. "How does seven-thirty sound to you? I'll need to make a run for the movies. Want to trust my judgment at the video store or do you have any suggestions? And hey, what are you doing about dinner?"

"I thought I'd take care of it. How do you feel about Chinese?" he replied nonchalantly.

"Really?" I asked again, impressed. All this and he was a gourmet cook, too?

"Sure. You do have a phone, don't you? I can order with the best of them."

And there it was. Dinner and a movie. At my place. My heart was pounding. I hurriedly checked to make sure my boss had gone for the day, and then left early myself. Hell, it was Friday. With lightning speed

I rendered the apartment, and then myself, moderately presentable. He arrived right on time, wheeling over my threshold with an easy grin that sprinkled goosebumps across my arms. "Nice place."

"Thanks. I like it well enough," I said. "Listen, do you want to just eat in here?" I asked, gesturing to the couch and coffee table. "I have a small table in the kitchen, but—" I could navigate it okay, but being a cerebral palsy walkie, even when you use a stick, is a whole different game from being a wheelie with a chair to cope with, and the kitchen was narrow and weirdly shaped.

"I think this will be fine," he said. "If your kitchen has the same layout as Jane's, we'll be happier in here." Of course. He probably visited Jane more often than I did. I was amused for a moment at the idea of him spending so much time in an apartment practically identical to mine, just three floors up.

"Well, I guess you probably already know where everything is, then, don't you," I chuckled.

"Pretty much," he replied, wheeling further into the room and deserting his chair for the couch without a moment's hesitation, clearly at home with the setting. I crossed the room and sat beside him, dropping the takeout menu for the upscale Chinese place a few blocks away in his lap and gesturing to the phone on the coffee table next to where he sat. He phoned in an order of General Tso's chicken, one order of shrimp lo mein, and some hot and sour soup, and informed me as he hung up that they were having a busy night, so we'd have about an hour and a half to kill.

I opened my mouth to ask him what he'd like to do while we waited. And then those green eyes caught me, and I decided right then and there exactly what I wanted to do with the time before our dinner arrived.

"Has anyone ever told you what beautiful eyes you have?" I asked, my voice soft.

I didn't really wait for a reply. I just leaned forward and hoped for the best, all the while expecting the worst. Our lips met. I had definitely gotten the best. He did not pull away—in fact, he leaned into the kiss eagerly, encouraging me. My mind began to race, questioning whether I was pushing him, whether I had forced the issue, whether I had this and that and the other, until at last the voice of reason cut in. *Oh, just shut up and fuck him.*

Okay, so maybe it wasn't entirely reason talking, but it was a very agreeable voice nonetheless. I broke the kiss somewhat reluctantly and moved even closer. I looked up to assess his reaction and found a bright smile spreading across his face. God, that smile. Warmth flooded through me as I looked at him. Something desperate awakened within me, not just between my legs but in my whole body, begging for him. I wrapped my arms around his neck and nuzzled for a moment, welcoming the feel of his skin against mine before allowing my tongue to snake out of my mouth to taste him for the first time.

I could tell that he hadn't been expecting it. He seemed at once excited and apprehensive, his body stiffening in response to my touch. I moved away slightly and looked into his face, reading his expression, which told me roughly what I expected it would. Gently, I leaned forward again and snuggled against his chest, taking one hand. He seemed to relax, and I smiled to myself as I listened to his heartbeat through his shirt. It was somewhat quick, but slowing down.

I closed my eyes for a moment and drifted, thinking about how my heart had raced just like Michael's as I lay atop the covers of Kyle's bed in the sticky August heat, the city pressing down around us making us crazy with lust. I had been so scared Kyle would be like the others who'd been with me that I flinched as he put a hand against my bare shoulder. Kyle had shifted suddenly, looking almost hurt. He spoke so quietly as he asked me what was wrong that I almost didn't hear him at all, and then I was in his arms completely, just being held and feeling safe. When I looked into his eyes then, I knew he would not be like the others, that I wasn't just a crippled girl spaz novelty fuck or a charity case. Something broke open inside me and I cried. But it was a good cry, a wonderful cry. His hands were warm and comforting on my skin as he and I began to learn each other's bodies, and I realized suddenly that he was enjoying every single inch of my skin. He genuinely liked it, each stroke of my hands, even with their tremor, every bend and curve of my body. The look on his face told me so. I was suddenly free. I knew that Kyle was different, because he loved me. Or at least I had thought I'd known that.

I nuzzled Michael's chest, kissed him under the chin, still musing. *Jesus Christ, girl, the last person you should be thinking about right now is Kyle Barnes.* Well, maybe not. I realized exactly why I had thought of Kyle, the man that I had almost married a year and a half ago. No matter what had happened between us near the end, Kyle had helped me to love myself. We had made magic. And tonight, that was exactly what I wanted to do. Michael deserved every good thing that Kyle had ever given me, and more. I looked up into his eyes as I thought of all that I could teach him, all that he had to show me, everything we could do together.

"Have you ever done this before?" I asked quietly, anticipating the answer which didn't come until I raised my head and looked up again into those big green eyes, filled with lust and fear. "Okay. It's okay. We'll go as slow as you want," I smiled, and lowered my face against his chest, holding him close. I continued in a soft whisper, running a few fingers lightly up and down his shirtfront. "I didn't mean to freak you out. I just . . . " Deciding to simply be honest, I offered sheepishly, "It's been a long time," laughing uneasily.

Suddenly, I was worried that I had ruined it—I had pushed him, and he had every right to be uncomfortable. I swallowed hard. "Look, I'm really sorry," I said after a pause, "I know how it is, how you feel. It's scary. They keep telling you . . . "

"That I shouldn't worry about this. I should concentrate on something else. Live my life and avoid *complications,*" he finished for me with a bitterness that sharpened into anger.

"Yeah," I smiled forlornly. "Yeah. I got that, too." My voice brightened as I did my best to reassure him. "But they're wrong. It doesn't have to be like that, Michael. You don't have to be afraid. I swear. They're wrong," I repeated emphatically. But I knew he would ultimately just have to trust me. It's tough to assimilate the fact that you've been lied to your whole life. It takes time. I should know.

His eyes were wet and uncertain as he considered what I had said, testing this new truth for loopholes, doubt and hope mingling in his gaze. Finally, with a weak smile, he spoke. "It's really goddamn easy for the doctors to say 'just ignore it, you'll be fine,' you know. It's not as if they have to follow their own advice."

I laughed, probably a little too loud, and realized there were tears in my own eyes. "Yeah . . . " I whispered, and I lay back against his chest, tracing lazy circles over the fabric of his T-shirt. I would've been content to stay like that, right there, all night. I had missed that feeling.

But now he was agitated. With the possibilities I'd offered had come a storm of new, overwhelming feelings, and he squirmed slightly beneath me. "So, can I . . . " he began, slightly uncomfortable. "Do you still want . . . ?"

I was suddenly reminded of a throbbing between my thighs which answered his question completely. "Hell, yes," I replied emphatically.

"Me too," he grinned, but his eyes betrayed his lingering unease. He watched me quietly again for a moment and I waited patiently. Finally, he spoke, an apologetic look framing his features. "I've got no idea what to do. Will you show me?"

"Sure, but I guess I'll have to cancel my dinner date with the Pope," I joked gently, hoping to put him at ease. "Hey. Don't worry." I ran a tentative hand over his shirt, and he smiled, but his lips were tight. "Relax. It makes it all a lot more fun," I confided. Then I licked my lips and winked at him as I eyed the sensitive flesh of his neck.

I again flicked my tongue against his smooth flesh. This time he was ready, and he melted into my touch. His pulse was already racing, and his eyes held a certain urgency. I stroked his sand-colored bangs with one hand to let him know that I understood, that I felt it too, but I would not rush through this. Not tonight. Not with him.

I began to suck delicately at the bit just above his Adam's apple, running my tongue slowly up and down in small movements, then a little bit faster, a little bit broader. I worked his shoulders with two hands, trying to relax him further, as I caressed his face and neck gently with my tongue and lips. His scent, musky with a faint hint of sweat, filled my nostrils, and I breathed deeply, letting it intoxicate me. The room seemed much brighter now than it had been only a moment ago, and again I marveled at the gorgeous glow of his green eyes, the softness of his skin.

I made my way along his neck and upward, across his right cheek, feeling the slight pricks of five o'clock shadow against my lips. He made a low moaning sound that sent a ripple of satisfaction through me as I teased his ear with a soft stream of breath, then nibbled the lobe. It encouraged him, and he reached for me, but I shook my head slightly and he stopped. I was enjoying this enough as it was. I wanted to focus on making sure he would have good memories of this night for a long, long time.

I moved down his cheek, across his chin, up and to the other ear, and I heard him draw in his breath sharply in anticipation. I learned the contours of the inside of his ear with delicate, probing licks, and as his shoulders at last relaxed, I moved my hands downward, over his nipples, rubbing in slow, soft circles until they stiffened into hard points. I trailed a few gentle fingers up and down his sides and listened as his breath quickened again, energizing me. Something inside me called out: *more, now.* I moved again toward his lips and took his tongue into my mouth, my own breath coming faster as I relished the heat of the kiss.

I was impatient. I wanted his hands on me, all over me, inside me. But I knew that there was more to be done. It was my turn, now, to share what I had learned, to bring him into the world of his body and its pleasures. I snaked my hands under his shirt, lifted it up over his head, and began again to gently caress his sides. He shivered under my hands and closed his eyes while I coaxed him into lying back on the sofa, maneuvering his legs from the floor to the cushions. In another moment his shoes were off, but he was sitting up, impatient, pulling me toward him, need making him restless. I leaned in for another kiss and managed to lay him down again, stroking his hair gently with one hand, tracing his cheekbone with the other. "Relax," I said as I broke the kiss, "I'm not going anywhere. I'm taking my time, that's all. We'll get there eventually. I'm just enjoying you," I grinned at him.

It was the right thing to say. He relaxed, blissful against the cushions, and closed his eyes, a soft sigh escaping his lips. I kissed his neck again, using my hands to trace the sides of his neck, up and down, delicate. When I reached the very bottom, where his neck and shoulder met, on the left side, he shivered slightly, and I grinned, teasing the spot gently with my tongue. His eyes popped open in surprise, lips parted, breath quickening. I would have to remember that spot.

I turned my attention to his arms, to the strongest muscles in his body, the ones that took the brunt of his day-to-day. I began again at his shoulders, kneading and stroking, and then ran my fingers lightly along each one several times, a teasing, yet persistent motion, aware that the lightest touches can elicit the best response. His breaths came more quickly now, and with each one a very soft moan which was nearly a sob. As my fingers played along the inside of each arm, his back arched toward me and I knew that he was ready. His eyes were clamped shut and his forehead creased with effort as he let out a long, low moan, sending a thrill of excitement through me. *So this is what it's like to be the seductress,* I thought, and grinned.

Knowing how close he was, I ran my tongue down along the spot I had found earlier, and worked open the buckle of his belt. He panted and strained toward me as I exposed his pale thighs. It wasn't until I laid a hand against his cool flesh that he realized his legs, scrawny and emasculate, were bared and clearly visible. I felt him leaning forward, and I pulled away. He was watching me with pain in his eyes.

"What's wrong?" I asked gently, stroking his cheek.

"My legs. . ." he trailed off sadly. The look on his face brought a lump to my throat. I thought back to the previous evening, when I had dressed in an ankle-length skirt to cover my own legs, my own blemished, vulnerable flesh. I understood all too well. I tried to convey the empathy I felt in my voice. "Oh, Michael, they're fine . . . you're beautiful. All of you." I placed a soft kiss on his lips and our eyes met.

We studied each other until he was sure I meant what I said, and relief flooded his features. Finally, with his eyes shining, he whispered, "I'm not the only beautiful one."

I beamed, feeling myself blush and not really caring. "So . . . " I prompted, placing my hands on his thighs. This time, he leaned forward to help remove the rest of his clothes. "Relax, I've got it," I assured him, but not before stealing another kiss.

With his clothes in a neat pile at the foot of the couch, I began to knead the outsides of his thighs, moving down both legs slowly, then back up again. "How's that?" I asked, and was pleased to see him smiling.

"How about this?" I leaned down and ran my tongue from groin to knee, down one thigh and up the other. He was suitably surprised—and aroused. Trembling beneath my tongue, his lips parted in another long low moan, this one with a harsher note in it, something carnal and demanding. I stroked one leg soothingly in response and then took a moment to pull off my clothing. Before he had opened his eyes I sat astride him and guided him inside me. I took both of his hands, bringing one toward my chest and settling the other against my clit, then guiding one finger in a minute circular motion.

He seemed relieved and excited. My pulse quickened and my cheeks flushed at the feel of his hands caressing my skin. I steadied myself, one hand gripping the back of the couch, and rocked up and down against him in time with his caresses. We fit together perfectly, and I at last let out a moan of my own, reveling in the feel of him inside me, straining for everything he could possibly get, everything we could possibly share. Again and again we rose and fell in unison. My legs were on fire from the effort—my tight, uncooperative thigh muscles really weren't engineered for that sort of thing, and they screamed in protest—but somehow I managed, again and again, until with one last sighing moan he came to the edge. Feeling him swell inside me, hearing the sweet note of fulfillment in his voice, I joined him with a feeling of triumph as we went over together.

Spent and contented, I leaned forward into his arms. He held and kissed me and murmured my name again and again as if in disbelief. At last my breathing slowed.

"So, beautiful, how was it?"

"Perfect," he whispered. Beaming, I lay against him, listening to his heartbeat and his breathing.

The doorbell rang, jolting me out of my reverie, my head shooting up. "Oh, shit!" I yelped. Michael gave a teasing little wave as I slipped off of the couch and made my way into the bedroom on legs made all the more awkward and wobbly by the recent exertion, hollering "just a minute!" in the direction of the front door.

I managed to get into my robe and grab the cash I'd set by the door. Heart still pounding, I opened the door and retrieved the food with a muffled "Sorry about that." As the delivery guy handed me the food and began to count my change, I overbalanced, suddenly reeling with the all too familiar sensation of being about to topple over. I grabbed the wall to steady myself, managing not to fall onto the flustered deliveryman. From the look on his face, I was sure he thought I'd gotten completely plastered, to the point where I was barely able to stand, and forgotten I'd ordered dinner at all. But at least that was probably all he suspected. At last the door was closed again and Michael and I burst into hysterical laughter, both of us far too familiar with other people's stupid presumptions to find them anything but laughable.

"Hungry?" I asked.

His eyes met mine, then he smiled eagerly as they moved down over my body, then back up again to my face, sending a small, beautiful shiver down my spine. "Starving," he said.

With a ceremonious flourish, I deposited the untouched food in the fridge, and we proceeded into the bedroom.

R. GAY
A COOL DRY PLACE

Yves and I are walking because even if his Citröen were working, petrol is almost seven dollars a liter. He is wearing shorts, faded and thin, and I can see the muscles of his thighs trembling with exhaustion. He worries about my safety, so every evening at six, he picks me up at work and walks me home, all in all a journey of twenty kilometers amid the heat, the dust and the air redolent with exhaust fumes and the sweet stench of sugarcane. We try and avoid the crazy drivers with no real destination who try to run us off the road for sport. We walk slowly, my pulse quickening as he takes my hand. Yves's hands are what I love best about him; they are calloused and wrinkled, the hands of a man much older than he is. At times, when he is touching me, I am certain that there is wisdom in Yves's hands. We have the same conversation almost every day—what a disaster the country has become, but we cannot even muster the strength to say the word "disaster" because such a word does not aptly describe what it is like to live in Haiti. There is sadness in Yves's face that also cannot be aptly described. It is an expression of ultimate sorrow, the reality of witnessing the country, the home you love, disintegrating around you. I often wonder if he sees such sorrow in my face, but I am afraid to look in a mirror and find out.

We stop at the market in downtown Port-au-Prince. Posters for

Aristide and the Family Lavalas are all over the place, even though the elections, an exercise in futility, have come and gone. A vendor with one leg and swollen arms offers me a box of Tampax for twelve dollars, thrusting the crumpled blue and white box toward me. I ignore him as a red-faced American tourist begins shouting at us. He wants directions to the Hotel Montana, he is lost, his map of the city is wrinkled and torn and splotched with cola. "We are Haitian, not deaf," I tell him calmly and he relaxes visibly as he realizes that we indeed speak English.

Yves rolls his eyes and pretends to be fascinated with an art vendor's wares. He has very little tolerance for "fat Americans." Just looking at them makes him feel hungry and feeling hungry reminds him of the many things he tries to ignore. Yves learned English in school, but I learned from television: *I Love Lucy*, *The Brady Bunch*, and my favorite show, *The Jeffersons*, with the little black man who walks like a chicken. When I was a child, I would sit and watch these shows and mimic the actors' words until I spoke them perfectly. Now, as I tell the red-faced man the wrong directions, because he has vexed me by his mere presence in my country, I mouth my words slowly, with what I hope is a flawless American accent. The man shakes my hand too hard, and thrusts five gourdes into my sweaty hand. Yves sucks his teeth as the man walks away and tells me to throw the money away, but I stuff the faded bills inside my bra and we continue to walk around, pretending we can afford to buy something sweet or something nice.

When we get home, the heat threatens to suffocate us. The air conditioning is not working because of the daily power outages, so the air inside is thick and refuses to move. I look at the rivulets of sweat streaming down Yves's dark face and I want to run away to some place cool and dry, but I am not sure that such a place exists anymore. My mother has prepared dinner, boiled plantains and *griot*, grilled cubes of pork. She is weary, sweating, slouched in a chair. She doesn't even speak to us as we enter, nor do we speak to her because there is nothing any of us can say to each other that hasn't already been said. She stares and stares at the black-and-white photo of my father, a man I have little recollection of because he was murdered by the Ton Ton Macoute, the secret military police force, when I was only five years old. Late at night, I am plagued by memories of my father being dragged from our home and beaten as he was thrown into the back of a large green military truck. And then I feel guilty because, regardless of what he suffered, I think that he was the lucky one. Sometimes, my mother stares at the picture so hard, her eyes glaze over and she starts rocking back and forth and it is as if he is dancing her across the small space of our kitchen the way he used to. In those moments, I look at Yves. I know that should anything happen to him, it will be me holding his picture, remembering what was and will never be, and I have a clear understanding of a woman's capacity to love.

We eat quickly and afterward, Yves washes the dishes outside. My stomach still feels empty. I rest my hand over the slight swell of my belly. I want to cry out that I am still hungry, but I don't because I cannot add to their misery with my petty complaints. I catch Yves staring at me through the dirty window as he dries his hands. He always looks at me in such a way that lets me know that his capacity to love equals mine: eyes wide, lips parted slightly as if the words "I love you" are forever resting on the tip of his tongue. He smiles, but looks away quickly, as if there is an unspoken rule forbidding such minor demonstrations of joy. Sighing, I rise and kiss my mother on the forehead, gently rubbing her shoulders. She pats my hand and I retire to the bedroom Yves and I share, waiting. It seems like he is taking forever, and I close my eyes, imagining his thick lips against my collarbone and the weight of his body pressing me into our mattress. Sex is one of the few pleasures we have left, so I savor every moment we share before, during and after. It is dark when Yves finally comes to bed. As he crawls under the sheets, I can smell rum on his breath. I want to chastise him for sneaking away to drink but I know that a watery rum and coke is one of the few pleasures he has for the savoring. I lie perfectly still until he nibbles my earlobe.

Yves chuckles softly. "I know you are awake, Gabi."

I smile in the darkness and turn toward him. "I always wait for you."

He gently rolls me onto my stomach and kneels behind me,

removing my panties as he kisses the small of my back. His hands crawl along my spine, and again I feel their wisdom as he takes an excruciating amount of time to explore my body. I arch toward him as I feel his lips against the backs of my thighs and one of his knees parting my legs. I try and look back at him but he nudges my head forward and enters me in one swift motion. I inhale sharply, shuddering, a moan trapped in my throat. Yves begins moving against me, moving deeper and deeper inside me and before I give myself over, I realize that the sheets are torn between my fingers and I am crying.

Later, Yves is wrapped around me, his sweaty chest clinging to my sweaty back. He holds my belly in his hands and I can feel the heat of his breath against the back of my neck.

"We should leave," he murmurs. "So that one day, I can hold you like this and feel our child living inside of you."

I sigh. We have promised each other that we will not bring a child into this world, and it is but one more sorrow heaped onto a mountain of sorrows we share. "How many times will we have this conversation? We'll never have enough money for plane tickets."

"We'll never have enough money to live here, either."

"Perhaps we should just throw ourselves in the ocean." Yves stiffens and I squeeze his hand. "I wasn't being serious."

"Some friends of mine are taking a boat to Miami week after next."

I laugh rudely because this is another conversation we have had too often. Many of our friends have tried to leave on boats. Some have made it, some have not, and too many have turned back when they realized that the many miles between Haiti and Miami are not so small as the space on the map. "They are taking a boat to the middle of the ocean, where they will surely die."

"This boat will make it," Yves says confidently. "A priest is traveling with them."

I close my eyes and try to breathe, yearning for just one breath of fresh air. "Because his kind has done so much to help us here on land?"

"Don't talk like that." He is silent for a moment. "I told them we would be going too."

I turn around and try to make out his features beneath the shadows. "Have you taken complete leave of your senses?"

Yves grips my shoulders, to the point of pain. Only when I wince does he loosen his hold. "This is the only thing that does make sense. Agwe will see to it that we make it to Miami, and then we can go to South Beach and Little Havana and watch cable TV."

My upper lip curls in disgust. "You will put your faith in the same god that traps us on this godforsaken island? Surely you have better reasons."

"If we go we might know, once in our lives, what it is like to breathe."

My heart stops and the room suddenly feels like a big echo. I can hear Yves's heart beating where mine is not. I can imagine what Yves's face might look like beneath the Miami sun. And I know that I will follow him wherever he goes.

When I wake, I blink, covering my eyes as cruel shafts of sunlight cover our bodies. My mother is standing at the foot of the bed, clutching the black-and-white photo of my father.

"Mama?"

"The walls are thin," she whispers.

I stare at my hands. They appear to have aged overnight. "Is something wrong?"

"Gabrielle, you must go with Yves," she says, handing me the picture of my father.

I stare at the picture, trying to recognize the curve of my eyebrow or the slant of my nose in his features. When I look up, my mother is gone. For the next two weeks I work and Yves spends his days doing odd jobs and scouring the city for supplies he anticipates us needing. I feel like there are two of me; I go through the motions, straightening my desk, taking correspondence for my boss, gossiping with my coworkers while at the same time I am day dreaming of Miami and places where Yves and I are never hungry or tired or scared or any of the other things we have become. I tell no one of our plans to leave, but the part of me going through the motions wants to tell everyone I

43

see in the hopes that perhaps someone will try and stop me, remind me of all the unknowns between here and there.

At night, we exhaust ourselves making frantic love. We no longer bother to stifle our moans and cries and I find myself doing things I would never have considered doing before; things I have always wanted to do. There is a certain freedom in impending escape. Three nights before we are to leave, Yves and I are in bed, making love. We are neither loud nor quiet as, holding my breasts in my hands, I trace his muscled calves and dark thighs with my nipples, shivering because it feels better than I could ever have imagined. Gently, Yves places one of his hands against the back of my head, urging me toward his cock. I resist at first, but he is insistent in his desire, his hand pressing harder, fingers tangling in my hair and taking firm hold. In the dim moonlight, I stare at his cock for a few moments, breathing softly. It looks different to me, in this moment, rigid and veined, curving ever so slightly to the right. I part my lips, licking them before I kiss the strangely smooth tip of his cock. His entire body tenses, Yves's knees cracking from the effort. I pretend that I am tasting an exotic new candy, slowly tracing every inch of him with my tongue. I drag my teeth along the thick vein that runs along the dark underside of his cock. My tongue slips into the small slit at the head. He tastes salty, yet clean, and my nervousness quickly subsides. I take Yves's throbbing length into my mouth. It becomes difficult to breathe, but it also excites me, makes me wet as he carefully guides me, his hands gripping harder and harder, his breathing faster.

Suddenly, he stops, roughly rolling me onto my chest, digging his fingers into my hips, pulling my ass into the air. I press my forehead against my arms, gritting my teeth, and I allow Yves to enter my darkest passage, whispering nasty words into the night as he rocks in and out of my ass. At once I feel so much pleasure and so much pain and the only thing I know is that I want more—more of the dull ache and the sharp tingling just beneath my clit, more of feeling like I will shatter into pieces if he inches any further. More. At the height of passion, Yves says my name, his voice so tremulous it makes my heart ache. It is nice to know that he craves me in the same way I crave him, that my body clinging to his is a balm.

Afterward, we lie side by side, our limbs heavy, and Yves talks to me about South Beach with the assurance of a man who has spent his entire life in such a place; a place where rich people and beautiful people and famous people dance salsa at night and eat in fancy restaurants overlooking the water. He tells me of expensive cars that never break down and jobs for everyone; good jobs where he can use his engineering degree and I can do whatever I want. And he tells me about Little Haiti, a neighborhood just like our country, only better because the air conditioning always works and we can watch cable TV. Cable TV always comes up in our conversations. We are fascinated by its excess. He tells me all of this and I can feel his body next to mine, tense, almost twitching with excitement. Yves has smiled more in the past two weeks than in the three years we have been married and the twenty-four years we have known each other, and I smile with him because I need to believe that this idyllic place exists. I listen even though I have doubts, and I listen because I don't know quite what to say.

The boat will embark under the cover of night. On the evening of flight, I leave work as I always do, turning off all the lights and computers, smiling at the security guard, telling everyone I will see them tomorrow. It is always when I am leaving work that I realize what an odd country Haiti is, with the Internet, computers, fax machines and photocopiers in offices, and the people who use them living in shacks with the barest of amenities. We are truly a people living in two different times. Yves is waiting for me as he always is, but today, he wears a nice pair of slacks and a button-down shirt and the black shoes he wears to church. This is his best outfit, only slightly faded and frayed. The tie his father gave him hangs from his left pocket. We don't talk on the way home. We only hold hands and he grips my fingers so tightly that my elbow starts tingling. I say nothing, however, because I know that right now, Yves needs something to hold on to.

I want to steal away into the sugarcane fields we pass, ignoring the old men, dark, dirty and sweaty as they wield their machetes. I want to find a hidden spot and beg Yves to take me, right there. I want to feel the soil beneath my back and the stalks of cane cutting my skin. I want to leave my blood on the land and my cries in the air before we continue our walk home, Yves's seed staining my thighs, my clothes and demeanor hiding an intimate knowledge. But such a thing is entirely inappropriate, or at least it was before all this madness began. My face burns as I realize what I am thinking and I start walking faster. I have changed so much in so short a time.

My mother has changed as well. I would not say that she is happy, but the grief that normally clouds her features is missing, as if she slid out of her shadow and hid it someplace secret and dark. We have talked more in two weeks than in the past two years, and while this makes me happy, it also makes me sad, because we can never make up for the conversations we did not have and soon cannot have. We will write, and someday Yves and I will save enough money to bring my mother to us in Miami, but nothing will ever make up for the wide expanse between now and then.

By the time we reach our home, Yves and I are drenched in sweat. It is hot, yes, but this is a different kind of sweat. It reeks of fear and unspeakable tension. We stare at each other as we cross the threshold, each mindful of the fact that everything we are doing, we are doing for the last time. My mother is moving about the kitchen, muttering to herself. Our suitcases rest next to the kitchen table, and it all seems rather innocent, as if we are simply going to the country for a few days, and not across an entire ocean. I cannot wrap my mind around the concept of crossing an ocean. All I know is this small island and the few feet of water I wade in when I am at the beach. Haiti is not a perfect home, but it is a home nonetheless. I am surprised that I feel such overwhelming melancholy at a time when I should be feeling nothing but hope.

Last night, Yves told me that he never wants to return, that he will never look back. Lying in bed, my legs wrapped around his, my lips against the sharpness of his collarbone, I burst into tears.

"Chère, what's wrong?" he asked, gently wiping my tears away with the soft pads of his thumbs.

"I don't like it when you talk like that."

Yves stiffened. "I love my country and I love my people, but I cannot bear the thought of returning to this place where I cannot work or feel like a man or even breathe. I mean you no insult when I say this, but you cannot possibly understand."

I wanted to protest, but as I lay there, my head pounding, I realized that I probably couldn't understand what it was like for a man in this country, where men have so many expectations placed upon them that they can never hope to meet. There are expectations of women here, but in some strange way it is easier for us, because it is in our nature, for better or worse, to do what is expected of us. And yet, there are times when it is not easier, times like that moment when I wanted to tell Yves that we should stay and fight to make things better, stay with our loved ones, just stay.

I have saved a little money for my mother. It started with the five gourdes from the red-faced American, and then most of my paycheck and anything else I could come up with. This money will not make up for the loss of a daughter and a son-in-law, but it is all I have to offer. After we leave, she is going to stay with her sister in Petit Goave. I am glad for this, because I could not bear the thought of her alone in this stifling little house, day after day. I am afraid she would just shrivel up and die like that. I am afraid she will shrivel up and die, regardless.

I walk around the house slowly, memorizing each detail, running my hands along the walls, tracing each crack in the floor with my toes. Yves is businesslike and distant as he re-makes our bed, fetches a few groceries for my mother, hides our passports in the lining of his suitcase. My mother watches us but we are all silent. I don't think any of us can bear to hear the sound of one another's voices and I don't think we know why. Finally, a few minutes past midnight, it is time. My mother clasps Yves's hands between her smaller, more brittle ones. She urges him to take care of me, take care of himself. His voice cracks as he assures her that he will, that the three of us won't be apart long. She embraces me tightly, so tightly that again my arms tingle, but I say nothing. I hold her, kissing the top of her head, promising to write as soon as we arrive in Miami, promising to write every single day, promising to send for her as soon as possible. I make so many promises I cannot promise to keep.

And then, we are gone. My mother does not stand in the doorway, waving, as she might were this a movie. We do not look back and we do not cry. Yves carries our suitcases and quickly we make our way to a deserted beach where there are perhaps thirty others, looking as scared as Yves and I. There is a boat—large, and far sturdier than I had imagined, for which I am thankful. I have been plagued by nightmares of a boat made from weak and rotting wood, leaking and sinking into the sea, the hollow echo of screams the only thing left behind. Yves greets a few of his friends, but stays by my side. "We're moving on up," I quip, and Yves laughs, loudly. I see the priest Yves promised would bless this journey. He is only a few years older than us, so to me, he appears painfully young. He has only a small knapsack and a Bible so worn it looks like the pages might fall apart at the lightest touch. His voice is quiet and calm as he ushers us onto the boat. Below deck there are several small cabins, and Yves seems to know instinctively which one is ours. At this moment, I realize that Yves has spent a great deal of money to arrange this passage for us. I know he has his secret, but I am momentarily irritated that he has kept something this important from me. He stands near the small bed, his arms shyly crossed over his chest, and I see an expression on his face I don't think I have ever seen before. He is proud, his eyes watery, chin jutting forward. And I know that I will never regret this decision, no matter what happens to us, because I have waited my entire life to see my husband like this. In many ways, I am seeing him for the first time.

Little more than two hours after the boat sets sail, I am above deck, leaning over the railing, heaving what little food is in my stomach into the ocean. Even on the water, the air is hot and stifling. We are still close to Haiti, but I had hoped that the moment we set upon the ocean, I would be granted one sweet breath of cool air. Yves is cradling me against him between my bouts of nausea, promising that this sickness will pass, promising this is but a small price to pay. I am tired of promises, but they are all we have to offer each other. I tell him to leave me alone, and as his body slackens against me, I can tell he is hurt, but I have too many things happening in my mind to comfort him when I need to comfort myself more. I brush my lips across his knuckles and tell him I'll meet him in our cabin soon. He leaves, reluctantly, and when I am alone, I close my eyes, inhaling the salt of the sea deep into my lungs, hoping that smelling this thick salty air is another one of those things I am doing for the last time.

I think of my mother and father and I think that being here on this boat may well be the closest I will ever come to knowing my father, knowing what he wanted for his family. My head is splitting because my thoughts are thrown in so many directions. All I want is a little peace, and I never feel more peaceful than when I am with Yves. Wiping my lips with the back of my hand, ignoring the strong taste of bile lingering in the back of my throat, I return below deck to find Yves sitting on the end of the bed, rubbing his forehead.

I place the palm of my hand against the back of his neck. It is warm and slick with sweat. "What's wrong?"

He looks up, but not at me. "I'm worried about you."

I push him further onto the bed and straddle his lap. He closes his eyes and I caress his eyelids with my fingers, enjoying the curl of his eyelashes and the way it tickles my skin. He is such a beautiful man, but I do not tell him this. He would most likely take it the wrong way. At the very least, it would make him uncomfortable. It is a strange thing in some men, this fear of their own beauty. I lift his chin with one finger and trace his lips with my tongue. They are cracked but soft. His hands tremble but he grips my shoulders firmly. I am amazed at how little is spoken between us, yet how much is said. We quickly slip out of our clothes and his thighs flex between mine. The sensation of his muscle against my flesh is a powerful one that makes my entire body tremble.

I slip my tongue between his lips and the taste of him is so familiar and necessary that I am suddenly weak. I fall into Yves, kissing him so hard that I know my lips will be bruised in the morning. I want them to be. Yves pulls away first, drawing his lips roughly across my chin down to my neck, the hollow of my throat, practically gnawing at my skin with his teeth. I moan hoarsely, tossing my head backwards, a gesture of acquiescence and desire. My neck throbs and I know that here, too, there will be bruises. He sinks his teeth deeper into me and I can no longer perceive the fine line between pain and pleasure. But just as soon as I consider asking him to stop, he does, lathering the fresh wounds with the softness of his tongue, murmuring sweet and tender words. Such gentleness in the wake of such roughness leaves me shivering.

The weight of my breasts rests in Yves's hands, and he lowers his lips to my nipples, suckling them. He looks up at me as he suckles, and it is unclear whether this is a moment of passion or a moment of comfort for him . . . for me. And then I cannot look at him so I rest my chin against the top of his head, my arms wrapped around him, my hips slowly rocking back and forth. My cunt brushes along the length of his cock, hard beneath me. I am wet already, and I want him inside me, but I wait. This moment, whatever it is, demands patience. He turns our bodies so that I am lying on my back and slowly, almost too slowly, he draws his tongue along my torso, inside my navel, the round of my belly. He is reverent in his touch and I can feel the tension in my body easing away as I surrender my trust and fear and hope to this one man.

His hands massaging my thighs, Yves places a cheek against the soft, wiry patch of hair covering my mound. And then he is tracing the lips between my thighs with only one finger. His touch is tentative at first, and then it is possessive and insistent as he covers the most sensitive part of me with his mouth, tasting and teasing me with his tongue, that one finger sliding inside me so subtly that I gasp, and clench around him and hear a distant voice begging him for more. It is agonizing that at a time like this, Yves is making love to me in such a manner when all I want is him fucking me so hard that I feel everything and nothing at all. His tongue is moving faster, so fast that it feels like a constant, and then I cannot take it anymore.

"Fuck me," I say harshly, and he blinks, looking at me as if he, too, is seeing me for the first time.

"Oui, ma chère," he whispers, crawling up my body, kissing me as he slowly slides his cock, inch by inch, into the wet heat of my cunt.

Yves takes hold of my knees, spreading my legs wide and pushing them upward until they practically touch my face. I rest my ankles against his shoulders and shudder as he pulls his cock to the edge of my cunt and then buries himself to the hilt over and over again. I am intimately aware of his pulsing length; his sweat falling onto my body, into my eyes, mingling with mine; the tension in his body as I claw at the wide stretch of black skin across his back with my fingernails. Tomorrow, he, too, will have bruises. My cunt loosens around his cock and Yves groans, hiding his face in my armpit, trying to stay in control.

"Let go," I urge him.

Then, he is fucking me faster and harder, so much so that I cannot recognize him, and my chest heaves because I am thankful. A cry that has been trapped deep in my throat is finally released and the sound of it is peculiar. It is a sound that only a woman who has known what I have known can make. I can feel wetness trailing down the inside of my arm. It is Yves's tears. My thigh muscles are screaming, so I wrap my legs tightly around his waist. I am tender inside but I don't want Yves to ever stop, because with each stroke of his cock he takes me further away from the geography of our grief and closer to a cool dry place.

COMMUNION

What I wanted—now, today and regardless—wasn't unthinkable. Paul and I had both done the responsible thing by getting ourselves tested for STDs soon after we had spent our first latex-wrapped night together. I knew that neither of us was likely to pass a killer virus to the other.

But fear of the Other is beyond reason. I knew what he had been told about women like me, in my state of messy openness: we were unclean. Dirty for being a shiksa, a godless gentile, and even dirtier for being in that female state that no one of his parents' generation ever talked about openly, even though they all knew that women needed cleansing afterward.

"The devil's gateway" is what women were called in the Catholic tradition of my ancestors, and how much more hellish the witch-finders must have found us when we gushed red, the devil's color. That never stopped them from searching us out.

"I was giving you your space," Paul explained, trying to fathom my motives. He held me against his chest, a field of animal fur thinly covered by an old T-shirt. I inhaled the warm spice of his armpits. "I was respecting your connection to your moon energy. I know about these things."

I was tempted to tell him that everything he had ever been told about women was perfectly true. It would have been the opening lie in another relationship that would eventually starve to death, deprived of truth.

"My coven would approve," I told him, trying to keep the sarcasm out of my voice and ignore the hunger in my cunt. "They all try to meditate in the woods for five days whenever possible. I'm only telling you how I feel." I felt alone, as usual. The verbal slaps for my heresy rose up in my mind: *bloody bitch, traitor, fool.* This last would surely be the opinion of the priestess who had advised me of my spiritual obligation to withdraw from carnal things for a precious few days every month. At the time, I hadn't doubted her.

I had only one defense. "I feel what I feel," I sighed in his troubled face. "I'm more sensitive at this time of the month. I want everything more: food, water, sex, sleep, warmth when I'm cold. You're the one who wants your space."

Paul's classic features looked closed and hard. I felt no sympathy for his momentary resentment. A lifetime of rejection was churning my stomach and demanding expression. "Are you sure you're not disgusted?" I demanded. "You couldn't stand it, could you?"

In answer, he held me tighter. He kissed me with a soft but persistent pressure, sliding his hot tongue into my mouth. His heat and his taste made my legs weak, and I felt like moving my hips. His arms were tight around me, and I needed their strength.

Unexpectedly, Paul picked me up and bounced me onto the sofa. He began unbuttoning my blouse, revealing my naked breasts. My large pinkish-brown nipples were already hard.

He looked like a teenage boy who has been dared to do something reckless, who would rather die than chicken out. "So," he demanded, gently mocking, "you'll starve to death if you don't get it now?"

I could hear my clit answering yes. My swollen labia felt like the gateway to the heavy, sensitive land of my hungry guts. I wanted to be fed through every opening.

He wouldn't feed me until I gave him an answer. "I want you," I murmured to the hard outline in his pants. It jumped.

He pulled my skirt and panties down my legs as I raised my ass to make it easier. I lay naked on the clean and civilized upholstery, about to leave my mark on it. "Will you bring me a paper towel?" I asked him politely.

"No." He grinned like a wolf. "We can clean up later."

Carefully, I reached between my spread legs to find the brimming plastic container and pull it out of me. Exposed to daylight, my cup of ruby wine drooled onto the sofa and the carpet as I stretched out an arm to place it, like a centerpiece, on the coffee table. A shaft of late-day sunlight from between the curtains completed the effect.

Posing like the actor he is, Paul reached down for the cup. Fondling and raising it at the same time, he studied the shreds of tissue in the dark liquid before calmly—and a little theatrically—sinking a long tongue into it. For a moment, I couldn't breathe.

I felt his tongue sliding into my wet heat as it slid around the plastic rim of the cup, tasting my essential fluid. He savored each tongueful as though trying to guess the vintage. He accepted the taste of salt and iron as though he had been nourished by my body all his life. I suddenly understood that like me, this man had been afraid to show his wild face to a lover he didn't want to lose.

"Taste it fresh," I invited him, moving my hips. My womb was cramping, and the contractions sent echoes into my lower mouth; I could almost hear it speak. It, and I, wanted a full meal after the lean years of giving up this nourishment for the sake of one orthodoxy or another.

His tongue seemed to fill me, slippery and flexible as a curious eel. Two demanding fingers followed, searching for all the itchy places that longed to be scratched. His fingers tickled and teased and asked questions that needed answers. I stroked his hair, fighting off the urge to react too hard and too fast.

When he backed away, he was licking a mixture of fluids off his mouth. He shed his clothes like a man about to plunge heroically into raging water to find lost treasure. His impatient cock sprang into view as though searching for fresh air. My eyes met his before he lowered himself onto me with the practical grace of an explorer, and entered me all the way with one thrust. "All the way" was what we, both girls and boys, called this when I was in high school, suggesting travel, mystery, danger, discovery. All the way to heaven or to hell. All the way home.

He fucked me to a compelling beat that was clearly determined by some force beyond his consciousness or mine. Equally mindless (or mind-free), I squeezed and rocked and thrust in the vain hope of making it last, and last, and last.

But Paul had a plan; he was not going to come alone. Stroking my outraged clit, he let me know that he wanted a reaction soon, and would not give up until he got it. Then, holding my ass cheeks in both hands, he shot his own fluid into me, against my womb. Gasping like a drowning swimmer, I went over.

He sighed, lying peacefully, comfortably, on top of me. I stroked his back, loving its warm smoothness. When he muttered something into my neck, I couldn't hear the words and didn't think their exact meaning was important.

Rising up, he let me see that his cock had sprung back to life. It was streaked with watery red slime as though it had penetrated a ripe water-melon. He grasped it affectionately and looked at me. "I need your mouth, baby," he told me. He seemed to believe I had already con-sented by not refusing.

What the hell, I thought, *fair's fair*. I accepted the smooth, bursting head into my mouth, flicking it gently with my tongue like a baby kitten learning to wash itself.

Taking in more of him, I tasted our minerals, our metals, our acids and bases, all mixed into a sexual soup.

I sucked and nibbled, not just to please him but because I wanted to be filled wherever I was open. A few well-placed strokes of my tongue had him groaning and gasping. A few more made him thrust so hard that I had to move quickly to avoid gagging. In a second, a fountain was gushing over my tongue, sliding toward my throat. I swallowed, noting the distinct flavor of his seed. By such things could I know him.

Casually, as if by afterthought, he slid two fingers into my wettest, most open mouth. Inch by inch, he traced the folds inside me until he found a ticklish spot on the upper wall, just above the entrance to my womb. I flinched as though an unexpected finger had been pushed up my ass. Grinning, he used his other hand to act out my unspoken thought, exploring my tighter hole with his index finger.

Being fucked in stereo, in two places at once, felt overwhelming, and his wrist pressed maddeningly against my clit as his fingers danced on the ceiling of my wet cave. The orgasm that began gathering strength throughout my guts was like a wave that seemed likely to wash out all my self-control and common sense forevermore. My cautious mind said no, but all my nerve endings screamed yes. I convulsed in spasm after spasm, greedily clutching pleasure as though it might never come my way again.

As we sank back into our separate selves, I felt a cooling, staining pool spreading beneath me. The thought of permanent bloodstains on Paul's sofa both tickled and disgusted me: They would be permanent proof of my sluttiness, signifying bad housekeeping as well as reckless lust. Rust-brown stains would also prove my existence, like the most basic of graffiti: *Colleen was here.* My name means "young woman" in the abstract, like the Greek word "Kore," the maiden. I will always be Colleen, but my maidenhood disappeared long ago.

I realized that I could no more guess the future of this relationship than I could guess Paul's whole past history. Would I leave a permanent stain on his life or his heart, or be erased within a year? I decided that I could control the outcome by moving first.

"Colleen," he breathed into my nearest ear, "you don't have to clean it up yet. I want you again." My own smell wafted to my nose, and it was as rich as the scent of a compost heap, lobster shells and rusty nails after a rain. Periodically, not often, an incredible man wants me like this. And by ignoring advice given for the good of body and soul, I got him, got what I wanted. I felt as if I had fallen into heaven, and it felt like bloody time.

Anne Tourney

THE BOOK OF ZANAH

I will write the Book of Zanah for you
So that you never forget that you are my whore.
When I touch you again, you will come to life screaming,
My Lazarus cunt, my whore in waiting.

—Zanah I:1-2

I know what it's like to be Lazarus, in the hours before he was brought back to life. During the years that Malachi was in prison, I spent my evenings in a Lazarus sleep, floating in TV twilight as I watched the flickering shadows on my living-room walls. Slowly, silently, my cunt closed like a tomb. This can happen to a woman, when she's been waiting too long for some dark prophet to wake her from the dead.

I used to fantasize about Malachi's fierce body, confined behind steel and concrete. I used to imagine him pacing like a tiger in the prison yard, or lying on his bunk with his hands folded behind his head, his mind seething. That mind was a crucible of dreams, and in those dreams, I was his hot, wanton whore. In moments of self-pity I used to wonder which one of us had it worse—Malachi, being incarcerated, or me, being free, but dying from the inside out.

When I was a child in Sunday school, I assumed Lazarus had been overjoyed to be resurrected. As a grown woman, I began to suspect that he had mixed feelings about returning to the harsh world of the living. Then I got a call from Malachi's sister, and I realized I was going to learn exactly how Lazarus felt.

"Mal's coming home," Bethany announced. She was my oldest friend. "I thought you'd want to know."

"You mean he's out? Already?"

"Early parole. I'm picking him up tomorrow."

I couldn't speak.

"You still there?" Bethany asked.

"I'm here. I think."

"Don't worry, honey. It's been ten years, you know."

Ten years would mean nothing to Malachi. His name meant "God's messenger," and he had lived up to that title every day of his life. Malachi was going to give me a message, all right. But I wasn't ready to hear it.

I didn't want to think about how prison had changed him. It was sweeter to conjure up memories of the eighteen-year-old boy. As I lay in bed that night, I saw the teenage Malachi wading toward me through the rootbeer-colored water of the lake. I saw his solemn mouth and the raven sheen of his hair, and those black eyes that burned like eclipsed suns. I saw his tanned body gleaming as he stepped onto the shore. I saw the shaft of his cock arching against his belly, the crown streaming water. In my fantasies, Mal's skin was always streaming water.

> *Are you afraid of being immersed in me, my love?*
> *Are you afraid of going under, and never coming up?*
> *Water washed me clean of blood, but never of desire.*

In an old Whitman's Sampler box at the bottom of my cedar chest lay a bundle of folded papers. I didn't like to think of them as letters. Letters were packets of civilized communication; these pages held nothing but sexual insanity. They were the visions of some crazed demon, transcribed in Malachi's impeccable seminarian handwriting. I had thought about taking the letters to the police. But how could I explain why I'd read those pages until they fell apart in my hands?

I crawled to the foot of my bed and fished the chocolate box out of my cedar chest. I opened the box and pulled out the apocryphal scriptures known as the Book of Zanah. The oldest pages smelled of seasoned wood. When I first received them, they had smelled of cigarette smoke and something else—the male essence of their author. I didn't want Malachi's smell to linger on those papers, so I'd stored them in the chest. Still, I would press them to my nose now and then, just to make sure the cedar was doing its job.

I lay back down in bed, switched on the bedside lamp and settled under the blankets to read the scriptures again. Not that I needed to read them. I could have quoted them in my sleep.

First thing in the morning, I called the library. Bethany answered.

"I'm sick," I said." I can't come to work today."

"You're no sicker than I am. Get in here."

"I can't leave the house. Your brother is going to come looking for me."

"Mal hasn't even mentioned you."

"He hasn't?"

"Of course not. He just got out of prison. He'll be spending every free moment trying to get his life back together. You really think he's going to hunt you down like some maniac?"

"Well . . . I guess not."

"What happened between you and my brother? It was Bible camp, wasn't it? The summer you were both counselors, right before he went to seminary." Sparing the library patrons, Bethany lowered her voice. "You had sex, didn't you?"

I could have told Bethany that her brother and I did have sex. Lots of it. A three-week orgy of damp, sweaty, chigger-bitten lust, stolen in spare hours under the mulberry trees behind the camp kitchen. But I couldn't have told her that when I seduced him, I altered his destiny. When Malachi dropped out of seminary, I saw the first sign of what I'd done to him. But it wasn't until he was convicted of murder that the dark bird I'd released came home to roost.

Before that summer I never lusted after Malachi. Malachi was going to be a minister. More than that, he was rumored to have the gift of prophecy. My best friend's brother was far too weird—with his religious vocation and his academic brilliance and his alleged visions—to be boyfriend material.

61

Anne Tourney

Then I saw him naked at Bible camp.

When I caught Mal walking out of the lake, it was as if his body had been reborn in the water, remade somewhere in that slow-motion trek through the early morning fog. Watching him was like witnessing a baptism in reverse. I had gone down to the lake for a swim, but I never made it past the shore. I was too busy staring at Malachi, and his lean wet torso, and his ruddy divining rod of an erection. That organ did not belong to any scrawny teenager. That was a man's cock, fully hard and ready to do man-things.

As I stood there gawking, Malachi's gaze froze on me. I was wearing last year's bathing suit, now a size too small. Because it was so early, I had figured that there wouldn't be anyone around to see the way the suit rode up my crotch, or exposed my breasts right down to the crinkled edges of my nipples.

Later Mal would tell me that when he walked up the bank that morning, he hardly recognized me. With my hair falling down in ragged sheaves along my brown shoulders, my nipples poking through the worn fabric and my pussy bulging like a cut peach, I was Jezebel, Delilah—every temptress he'd been taught to fear. He stepped up to me wide-eyed, as if I had just burst into flame. A furious blush mottled his cheeks.

"Could you hand me my towel?" he asked. "It's sitting on those rocks behind you."

Without saying a word, I handed him my towel instead. As he rubbed his body dry, my eyes followed the trail of the white terrycloth. His skin was almost hairless, though the dripping black pelt around his cock was as thick as an animal's fur. I couldn't take my eyes off that cock. For the life of me, I can't explain why I did what I did next. I had never done anything like it, in reality or in my waking dreams.

I got down on my knees in front of my best friend's brother. As my kneecaps sank into the mud, I almost toppled. Malachi took hold of my shoulders. His cock was at my eye level. The rosy head wept a pearl. I had never seen an erect penis at close range, but I knew this must be a magnificent specimen. I had no idea what to do next. I kissed that cock out of sheer reverence and confusion.

62

Malachi gave a panicked cry. His body jerked wildly, then eased into a trembling stillness. His breath came in ragged bursts as his erection nudged its way between my lips. I had a few long seconds to taste him—lake water and salt and honey—before he exploded. As he came, he gave a shuddering groan, a guttural sound that sent a tremor of desire rippling through my gut. His come burbled over my lips like silky, soapy lava.

When he finally caught his breath, Malachi looked down at me. He cupped my cheeks in his hands and gazed at me as if my face were a ball of floating light.

"You're my whore," he said. His voice was soft with surprise.

When I saw you that day, Malachi wrote to me later from prison, *I understood what "flesh of my flesh" meant. I understood what it meant to "know" a woman in the biblical sense, because I knew you—I recognized you—with my body. The way I felt about you went way beyond lust. You were my desires incarnate. I wanted your flesh more than I ever wanted the body of Christ. Is there anything more blasphemous than the way I want you?*

A lover can tell you things about yourself that no one else knows. Malachi told me that my body—to my own eyes, too thin and lanky—was suffused with so much sensuality that my pores wept desire. That my flesh was luminous with lust. That the incandescent substance that made up my being was not just meat, but a soul in its own right, a piece of immortality. Malachi gave me a new name, because my old one didn't do justice to the woman I really was.

"Your new name is Zanah," he said. "That's Hebrew. It means to be a harlot, or a whore. That's what you are to me."

A whore? I was an honors student, president of the Latin club, Bible camp counselor. Not in a million years would I have thought of myself as a whore; I wasn't even in the running for the title of Town Slut. Yet somehow, when I was writhing naked under Malachi's body, the word felt right. It felt like what I was—if not to the world in general, then to him. To the world, I was quiet and modest and dry. To Malachi, I was ripe and lewd and wet.

He grabbed my pussy and squeezed the handful of flesh. "This pussy belongs to me. Those breasts belong to me. You're going to be my whore forever."

"Then you'll have to give up seminary, won't you?"

That was the first time I'd given voice to a feeling that had been growing inside me—a bitter clot born of confusion. Malachi fucked me till I couldn't remember my name, but he hadn't stopped acting right-eous around the campers. He said he worshipped my flesh, but he hadn't stopped praying to God. Every time he blessed the evening meal or led the campers in a hymn, I felt betrayed. How could he tell me that my pussy held his only salvation, yet still claim to uphold the First Commandment—*Thou shalt have no other gods before Me?*

"Of course I'm not giving up seminary. I'm going to be a minister."

"What will I be, then? A minister's whore?"

I laughed. Malachi didn't. Those glaring black eyes didn't belong to any gentle, picnic-blessing pastor. Even at eighteen, Malachi had eyes that were pure brimstone.

"Don't worry about what you'll be," Malachi said." You just be ready for me when the time comes."

I picked up one of the limp condoms we'd used and flung it as far as I could, as if I were throwing away the whole summer.

"Maybe I'll be ready for you. Maybe I won't. It depends on whether you decide to stop lying to yourself."

He looked at me for a long moment." Don't say things you don't mean."

"Go to hell."

I didn't mean that literally. But when it came to God and hell and sal-vation, Malachi inhabited a world of the literal. Every curse was as real to him as the sight of blood. He rolled away from me, sat up and pulled on his T-shirt and shorts. Then he scrambled to his feet and stalked away.

"Hypocrite!" I screamed at his retreating back. "If you loved me, you'd never go to seminary. You're just scared to admit you don't believe in God. All you believe in is my pussy!"

For a second he stood rigid, as if his muscles were absorbing my words like venom. Then he kept going.

Why couldn't Mal and I start a new religion? A religion of the flesh, in which the flesh was its own message—wasn't that what he had been building with me all summer? Even though he was my first lover, I knew what a rare gift he had. He gave me orgasms that sent my heart into paralysis, leaving me hovering for a few seconds until my pulse started up again, like a broken clock stuttering back to life. In those interstices of time, salvation did exist.

"See? You don't need to be born again," he told me, when I was coming down from one of those rapturous, heart-stopping spasms. "You only need to be born."

With those words he wiped out my baptism and all the salvation that Christ offered me, because according to what Malachi taught me that summer, the flesh held its own heaven.

After the day he walked away from me, Mal stopped meeting me out behind the kitchen. I spent hours alone in our spot under the trees, grinding mulberries into a blood-thick paste in my palm. I crouched behind a tree and watched him in his Old Testament classes. His coal-black eyes, eyes that used to burn for me, now burned for God again. The campers sat rapt through his study sessions. His descriptions of the blood and sex and beauty of the Bible were the next best thing to an afternoon at the movies. But more than that, the kids sensed a current of danger in Malachi, some fervid, barely contained electricity that sparked from his eyes.

The only reason I believed in God anymore was that He had become my rival. Back then, I didn't understand that God was the only thing keeping Malachi sane.

I lie awake all night with my eyes open. It's not because I'm afraid.

I'm a messenger, and a messenger can't afford to be afraid. I lie awake all night because I don't need sleep. I don't need food. My muscles feed on strange divinities. I am a messenger from your mind, Zanah. It's your voice telling me what to write. Your voice, the way it sounded when you lay beneath me. When these long years are over, you'll be lying beneath me again—right after you read the final chapter of the Book of Zanah.

I stayed home from work for the next three days, hiding in my little rented bungalow. Every few hours I would open the curtains and peer out the window. No sinister parolees haunted my porch. I kept the volume down on the TV set so I could hear any suspicious creaks or thuds, but the house was as quiet as an open grave.

Getting ready for bed, I watched my reflection in the bathroom mirror. My blood, like a thawing river, was starting to stir again. My cheeks and lips were flushed. My nipples grew whore-hard the instant I touched them. As I lay in bed, my hand buried between my thighs, I spun out one solitary orgasm after another and remembered the digging thrust of Malachi's tongue between my cunt lips. At the smallest sound, I held my breath until I was certain that danger had passed. You would have thought I expected Malachi to come storming into my bedroom like a furious angel, bursting with the pent-up need of ten years.

That wasn't what I expected—only what I wanted more than the continued beating of my heart.

"Well, well," Bethany said, when I came back to work on Friday. "Are you sure you'll be safe here at the reference desk?"

"I'm sorry, Beth. It's not my fault I'm scared."

Bethany scowled. "You don't need to be scared. My brother doesn't want to see you."

"What?"

"Malachi wants you to leave him alone."

"Me? Leave him alone?"

Beth must have seen my shock, because she took my hand and squeezed it.

"Yes, honey. Mal asked me to tell you not to go looking for him."

So Malachi didn't want to see me. There had been no need to hide. The Book of Zanah had been a feverish prison dream, not a prophecy of lust to be fulfilled. What did I want with a man like Malachi, anyway? I should find a decent, dependable lover. I didn't need a convict who wrote pages of rambling verses about me, verses in which my flesh held the light of immortality. Verses in which I became his one divinity, and he became mine.

The weeks passed. Here and there I heard scraps of gossip about Malachi, but in my mind he was still in prison—a prison of soul and bone. That was the Malachi who called to my body at night.

After Mal dropped out of seminary, he'd disappeared, at least in the town's estimation. In a town that took its religion seriously, his departure was considered a sure sign that Satan had overtaken his heart. I learned from Bethany that her brother had become a drifter, hopping freight trains across the country. The next thing we knew, he had been convicted of murder. Bethany wouldn't talk about the details, even to me, but word filtered down that the victim had been a hobo, and that Mal had stabbed him to death during an argument over a camp he'd staked out beside the railroad tracks.

No one in town could imagine Mal committing murder—no one but me. When he clutched my hips, the desire surging through his fingers was as raw as rage. Lying underneath him as he rammed into my body, I could barely meet his eyes. The heat in those eyes felt like a baptism of blood. His holiness wasn't sweet, or calm, or tame—it was a faith born of hellfire.

I gave up God for you, Zanah
Because there was nothing I wanted more than your flesh.
I walked through the desert, searching for you,
Following the dream of your red tent.

I killed a man when rage overcame me—
I killed him because I had lost my soul.

Soon after he was sentenced to prison, the verses started coming in the mail. Mal never asked me to respond. But each verse held a promise, or a threat, of what would happen when he finally got out of prison. I considered moving out of town, but somehow I couldn't leave. Day and night I felt Mal's desire engulfing me. If I left, I might never receive another one of his verses, in which my body was glorious in its immanence, terrifying in its transience.

Winter came. In those short, bitter days I dreamed of the sun-baked desert Malachi wrote about in the Book of Zanah. One night when I got home late from work, I looked at the front of my darkened bungalow and realized that an empty house is a desert of its own.

I went inside, locking the door behind me. A pool of lamplight warmed the foyer. My stomach turned to jelly. I never left that lamp on.

How could I have stepped through that door without knowing he was here? The whole house smelled of him: musk and brimstone, sweetened by leather and cigarette smoke. I pivoted silently on one heel and reached for the doorknob.

"Zanah?"

Zanah. Dear lord, the sound of that name still made me dissolve. His voice, like his scent, had grown richly bitter, deepened and roughened by hard time.

"Come here. Don't be afraid."

I turned and walked down the hallway. At the threshold of my bedroom, the male scent was so strong that I had to steady myself against the wall. When I entered the room, my blood turned to ice water. For a second I thought this night was about to go horribly wrong, because the man on the bed was not Malachi.

The man lying on my bed had long hair, as lustrous as a raven's wing. The black locks flowed across his shoulders and broad chest. He had a goatee that would have made him look like the devil, if those eyes hadn't done the job already. If not for those eyes, I never would have believed that this man was the Malachi I'd known at Bible camp.

He was all muscle now. Muscle carved in confinement, honed by anger and frustration. His pectorals bulged under a white cotton T-shirt, and his thighs, in faded jeans, were as thick as tree trunks. His corded arms were bent at the elbows, hands clasped behind his head. One of his legs was crossed casually over the other. The heels of his scuffed boots dug into my grandmother's quilt. I let my eyes drift up his calves and thighs, pausing before I got to the region below his belt buckle. I wasn't going to look there. Not yet.

"What took you so long to come home?" Malachi asked.

I couldn't answer at first. The words that filled my head came straight from the Book of Zanah: blood, desire, rage, love, fuck.

"My car's in the shop," I finally said." I had to wait for a ride."

"I've been waiting for you."

"What are you doing here?"

"I came to finish what I started."

"Finish what?"

Malachi shifted his body, unclasped his hands and picked up the old Whitman's Sampler box that lay on the bed beside him.

"This," he said.

"How did you know where to find that? You had no business—"

"Yes I did. I've been waiting ten years to show you the last chapter," he said.

"Maybe you waited too long."

He opened the box. His hands were knotted, the knuckles ribbed with scars and calluses.

"Writing this book saved my life. When I was hopping trains, half-crazy and not knowing where I was going, these visions were my only evidence that I still had a soul. When I was in prison, writing these verses let me keep my sanity."

"If you'd known what was good for you," I said, "you never would have left me that summer."

"Can't argue with that."

"And if you've been waiting so damn long," I sputtered, "then why the hell didn't you want to see me when you first got out of prison?"

"I had to get myself together first. Find a job, a place to live. I didn't want to show up on your doorstep like some pitiful jailbird." He rubbed the quilt beside him. "Come sit by me, Zanah. I want to touch you again."

My legs were so weak I thought my knees would buckle. I sank onto the bed. Mal put his arms around me and held me tight. When he was eighteen, he had smelled of mint toothpaste and shaving cream. Now he smelled of musk and leather, smoke and loss. I could feel the tension in his muscles, hear the dull thunder of his rushing blood.

"Are you ready to see that last chapter now?"

I nodded.

Mal rolled away from me and sat on the edge of the bed. He pulled off his T-shirt, revealing a heavily slabbed version of the chest I remembered from Bible camp. But this wasn't a boy's torso. A jagged white scar snaked across his ribs. A purple gouge adorned his left breast, as if someone had tried to carve out his heart. He shook his hair free of the T-shirt. Then he turned around, pulled his hair over one shoulder, and let me see his back.

I lost my breath.

The smooth expanse of skin was covered with words.

Rivers of words undulated across the lateral muscles, peaked along the ridge of his spine, and flowed down the other side. Line after line of cramped letters, tattooed in dark blue ink. Malachi must have bled for days under a needle so that he could wear that mantle of verses—not just the final chapter of his Book of Zanah but the whole thing, starting at the crest of his left shoulder and working its way down his waist. The final lines disappeared below his waistband.

My throat was so dry that it hurt to swallow. "I can't read the last lines. Unless you take your jeans off."

He pulled off his boots, then stood up and slipped out of his jeans.

I saw his cock, hard as jasper, rising out of the underbrush of his pubic hair. A whimper rose from my throat.

"Read the last verse," he said, his voice thick.

> The promise in your flesh is as old as life
> Zanah—my harlot, my whore.
> Raw, blind, and bleeding, I entered your tent
> You opened your arms, and welcomed me in,
> Saying, "I am your whore—my flesh is your soul."

I stared at the waves of sheer heresy that crossed his powerful back. He would be wearing that cloak of words on Judgment Day, if he still believed in such a thing.

"Aren't you afraid?" I asked.

"Of what?"

"Of God. Of damnation."

He stretched out on the bed beside me. Feeling the full, throbbing length of his naked body was more than I could bear.

"Your flesh is my God," he said. "As long as you love me, there's no damnation."

One of his hands slid under my skirt and parted my thighs. His fingers tugged at the soaking wet gusset of my panties. He turned me over on my back and propped himself up on one elbow. His hair fell like a black shawl, gold-fringed in the light of my bedside lamp.

"You took too long," I said. My voice sounded strangled. "I almost gave up waiting."

"But you didn't," he said. "Look at me."

For the first time that night I looked him straight in the face. It was a prophet's face—so dark and fierce, its angles sharpened by suffering. Ten years ago he had lain in exactly the same position, staring down at me in the shade of the mulberry trees. We'd been lifted out of time and dropped down a tunnel of pain, only to land here together on my grandmother's quilt. He touched my cheek.

"I thought I was lost, after I killed that man," he said. "I thought I wasn't ever going to find my way out of that wasteland. Prison didn't matter. Prison was nothing, compared to the hell in my head. My visions were the only thing that kept me going. You were waiting for me at the end of that desert, with your beautiful dark hair, and your soft mouth, and your flesh that's all mine."

He kissed me. His lips were cool and dry, but when I opened my mouth, his hot tongue writhed like a serpent.

"I want to be naked, too," I whispered.

Malachi unbuttoned my blouse, his fingers trembling as they worked the pearl buttons one by one. Then he unclasped the barrette at the back of my neck and loosened my hair.

"You look just like I imagined you," he said. "You look like my salvation."

He helped me slip out of my skirt, panties and bra, then cupped my breasts and suckled each nipple. His hands moved down to my belly and thighs, working my flesh as if he were molding me out of clay. Dizzy with desire, I saw red all around me, red like the walls of a harlot's tent. The light of my lamp was the desert sun outside those walls. The drumbeat of blood filled my ears, and I heard singing all around us, like a chorus of maidens. We had both been imprisoned for so long that tonight felt like nothing less than a wedding.

His callused fingers began strumming at the folds of my cunt. I ground my pussy against the heel of his hand, and before I knew it, I was climbing skyward. A cry flowed from my lips. I could feel my body coming to life—wave after wave of radiant life. Just as I peaked, he entered me hard and fast. I wrapped my legs around his waist and drew him deep inside me. I hadn't stopped coming. I wasn't ever going to stop coming.

Malachi's teeth clenched. His hair billowed like black sails in a storm as he pumped his hips against mine. All the anguish and shame of the past ten years were scorched into his eyes, but when he cried out in pleasure, the sorrow vanished from his face. The sharp furrows disappeared; his brow went smooth. I saw the eighteen-year-old Malachi gazing down at me again, his eyes soft with astonishment.

You're my whore.

What was it like for Lazarus after Christ brought him back to life? He must have seen all of creation transformed, a world incandescent. His body must have quaked with every small sensation. What is sex like for a woman who's been asleep for so many years? Like nothing less than a resurrection—like finding salvation in her own flesh.

PREGNANT PAUSE

He kissed me goodbye this morning, his hand on my Buddha belly. I spanked him, a mere tap, his left cheek vivid to my hand through his thin suit pants. "Promises, promises," he said, like he always did, but without his usual mocking tone.

The screen door closed between us. He took ginger steps down the driveway. Lately I'd been the one with a peculiar gait, so I savored the switch. I don't know whether he cocked his fanny and reached back to adjust his inseam for necessary comfort or for my viewing pleasure. I suspect both.

He didn't take the motorcycle, despite the clear weather. The vibrating saddle would've been too much after what I'd given him. Maybe I should have made him ride it, a throbbing, over-the-speed-limit memory enhancer, every bump and pothole a deep-seated reminder of my affection.

Usually he swings himself into the four-by-four in one smooth movement. He inhabits his body with macho grace and ease, whether in jeans, a suit or a skirt. Instead he scooched himself backward up onto the seat with awkward caution. Despite the glare of the morning sun on the windscreen, I spotted his ecstatic flinch as his ass made contact with the seat. Again, maybe the performance was just for my benefit. I didn't care. I appreciated the show. After all, I hadn't gotten to see much of his face the night before.

I confess. I am seven and a half months pregnant. And last night, I butt-fucked my husband.

I know. I need to learn to watch my language. My mother-in-law would be appalled.

Doggie-humping him in my gravid state wasn't easy. I struggled not to roll back on my butt like a wobbled Weeble, pulled out of him by the gravitational weight of my belly and the large mass of my ass, which had expanded as rapidly as my uterus. For leverage, I propped myself up against the bolster purchased for my prenatal yoga course. I wedged the firm pillow against the wall behind me and restrategized my rear-flank assault. I liked this pose much better than the bladder-strengthening asanas.

My husband was very accommodating in his movement and positioning. He had waited out the protracted abstinence of my pregnancy without complaint. I hadn't felt an erotic charge since I started throwing up the day after conception. I couldn't even see my pussy anymore, much less be in tune with it. No, my resolve to do this was to please him. To connect. To close the distance between us—when we hugged, we had to lean in over my protruding belly to kiss. More of a joke than sex, really. He'd deprived himself of masturbation for months, wanting the sympathy pain to bond us. Cut off from our shared sexuality, he was a phantom limb—with a raging itch. So now that I'd scratched his suppressed arousal, inflaming his mind's erotic rash, he wasn't about to give up over minor logistics. I couldn't see his face, but I knew he was in ecstasy.

The power of the fucking unleashed an anger which surprised me. His cock, his sperm, had transformed me, incapacitated me. Made me puke and waddle and swell. Made me a public artifact, people thinking they had the right to touch my ballooning belly as if it weren't my body, as if it weren't personal. Rammed me into a gender-specific role we'd spent our decade of marriage refuting, trading roles and holes once we crossed the bedroom threshold. Trapped me in the inexorable biology of my body, despite my having thwarted sexual expectation since saying, "I do." Made me helpless and vulnerable, needing seats on buses, assistance down stairs and a frigging potty break every three seconds. He had to drive me everywhere: once we pushed the seat back far enough to accommodate my girth behind the steering wheel, my feet didn't touch the pedals.

This thrust of my hard shaft in his tender ass—near-virginal after so much time—burst through months of built-up resentment like a pricked balloon. I was rough, not nice. I wielded my cock with no care, taking my hostility out on him.

He'd complained about my sissy dominance in the past. He said I twittered when I spanked, I didn't pinch or bite hard enough, my knots were too loose. Blah blah fucking blah. Well, he didn't bellyache last night. I was the boss, a queen bee with a personal grudge and a wicked stinger. There was no giddiness, no fear of hurting if I went too deep, too hard, too fast. I wanted him to pay for my suffering. One peep and he would have been grateful for too tame, too timid, too easy. Fuck him and his teasing. Wimp.

He howled. I can't think what else to call the noise he made. I don't think he knew what planet he was on, but for certain his mind was simultaneously concentrated on the small hole I violated and abused, and also far away, in a distant galaxy conjured by pain and pleasure. He protested a couple of times, but I told him without giggles to shut up and take it. He did. He needed to come. He was desperate for it, in fact. Wild for my hand.

I had trussed up his balls and cock in the O-ring he'd purchased at the hardware store. I'd had to get it on quick, he'd gotten hard so fast at the sight of me when he walked in the front door. I'd strapped on a major household appliance we'd never used before—a dildo we'd christened "Goliath" for good reason. He knew what the strap-on meant. I'd never had the guts to penetrate the man I love with something so ugly and stupendous. Getting the damn thing on with no waistline was a feat of genius; I could see only the swirled-purple tip over the Vesuvius of my abdomen. At the sight of the Corinthian column sprouting from below my belly, rooted in the curlicues of my pubic hair, his eyes went wide. But not as wide as his ass had to be to take it.

I'd buckled his collar on, too, the one that's always been a little too tight. I didn't attach a leash; I grabbed his hair. Usually I followed his cues even when he was mine to use and abuse. But not last night.

"No," I told him, just like I say it to the dog, firmly, and only once, as the obedience school trainer instructed, so he knew I meant it the first time. He reached for his cock. My husband, not the dog, that is, but what's the difference?

"No!"

He reached to tug at the collar. "No!"

He reached back for me. "No!"

He even said "please." He'd never said that before, not while on all fours. I always gave him what he wanted before he had to ask. But, *click*, I got it this time. He wanted it, yes, he needed it, oh, yeah, but he wanted to beg even more. My pliancy had always denied him part of this passion play. I decided to make him beg until he was hoarse. To provoke his pleas until his asshole was sore, so that he remembered this union of bodies for days. *Every time he sits, bends, walks, pees or shits, I told myself, the searing memory of the sex which created his discomfort will come back to him with a jolt. As it does to me.*

I'm aware that we looked ridiculous. I'm also aware that if the neighbors ever caught sight of us, Child Protective Services would be hauled in. The authorities would make advance plans to confiscate the baby (we've chosen not to know the gender; there'll be time enough for those expectations later). But they would have banished us from neighborhood Block Watch potlucks years ago if they had peered through our bedroom blinds. They wouldn't understand that this fucking helps ensure that we will still be together, husband and wife, man and husband, woman and wife, creatively intertwined till orgasm do we part, for this child's high school graduation.

This is a wanted pregnancy, long-awaited. Why else would I keep a stick I've peed on as a souvenir of one of the happiest days of my life? So I didn't expect to uncork anger—anger I'd hidden even from myself—as I both unplugged and corked *his* dam of frustration. Silently, a dune of resentment had built up inside me, keeping us apart as much as the sickness, the fragility, the fear, the doctor's cautions. Fucking eroded the barriers, brought me back to center point like a compass. Just as my physical body was off center, off balance, so was my mind, my perception of myself. I craved a good dose of yang for my yin. I needed his wide-open, vulnerable body splayed beneath me, just as I have been wide open and vulnerable ever since the missionary-position sex, lying with my ass hiked up on a pillow to aid the heroic journey of the sperm, that created this life inside me. I needed him trembling under my thrusts—my catharsis for having surrendered my body to an alien being.

A thrill of power coursed through my loins, power stripped from me when his invasive sperm rammed my passive egg. A vengeful, domineering, raw power, capable of sending him to the guillotine, the lions, the cross . . . stripped naked, tortured into humiliating public hardness, and on the verge of perpetually denied orgasm. The occasional Braxton Hicks contraction I'd experienced lately, my body preparing for labor, was nothing compared to the rocket-takeoff orgasm which suddenly hit me. He whimpered when I blasted off from his launch pad, jealous that I allowed myself the searing, keening pleasure I denied him.

Did I let him come? Heavens, no. I wanted to whack his piñata as long as possible before the candy tumbled out. As I write, I still haven't let him. I'll make him wait until I'm good and ready and in the mood . . . after he has enslaved himself enough to understand what it's like to invite a tadpole to morph inside you. Whether it's embryo- or woman-with-a-dick-sized, the control is complete.

Besides. He liked it.

I know from the wink, the sheepish grin he flashed me as he backed out of the driveway this morning. His wedding ring glinted in the sun as he waved goodbye. I waved back with placid, matronly affection, my ready-to-pop belly unmistakable through the screen door. It's been so long since I have seen him so glowing, so radiant . . . but they say that's what pregnancy will do for you.

Hanne Blank

LUST, DEBT AND A PRACTICAL EDUCATION

W hen it comes to love, the confessional is one of the most difficult edifices to inhabit. It's so much easier to stick to the present tense of the slippery rooms that my lovers and I create together, to remain in those palaces of moaning and biting and glad-hearted fucking, licking the salt and the come off of one another's bodies, than to set myself apart like this to try to recall the old, the long-broken, the shameful, the glorious, the once-upon-a-times and the might-have-beens.

For the sake of memory, though, and for the sake of love, it is sometimes good to spend time in confession—and if not for love, then at least for clarity. It is difficult to gain clarity where love is involved, and more difficult still when the matter at hand is lust, but sometimes the attempt at writing them down proves, in the end, the most fruitful part of the love itself.

I once wrote that lists were the pornography of history, so I cannot be so banal as to simply list my lovers. I've done it when asked, but people's reactions to the litany make me feel too much like Leporello, narrating Don Giovanni's *mille e tre* with his cruel, titillated leer. People are altogether too pleased by such impersonal epics of seduction. Instead, I will write about the first man who took me to bed, and what I found there.

I was eighteen then. A bit more than half my life ago, I was a virgin, whatever that really means. I wasn't in a particular rush to get laid, but then, I was (then as now, no?) fairly content to take advantage of what life might throw my way. So life threw me a Frenchman in his mid-thirties . . . but I begin to precede myself.

I left home young and moved to Europe, studying and traveling when I could, existing in a charmed bubble of stolen time, great art and fabulous bread, unconscious of my good fortune. How heady it was to be able to come and go as I pleased, no parents breathing down my neck, to be able to hop on a train and go to Paris, to Amsterdam, to Nuremburg or Nice.

It was a spring day in Nuremburg, the sun lambent and gently yellow on the old stone. I remember the walk down the river and across town to the museum of toys where I first met him. He noticed that my backpack was a Jansport, not a European make, and he struck up a conversation by asking me where I was from. I was looking into a case of little pull-toys at the time, the kind with a number of wheeled toy animals on a string, perhaps a mama duck and a line of baby ducklets following her, antiques or something, though I hardly remember anymore. When I looked up to see who was speaking to me, I met a glittering pair of hazel eyes framed by curls just starting to turn silver in places, and a cautious but warmly gorgeous smile that made me want to smile back. As genial and as much older as he was, he probably tripped every little Electra-complex switch in my psyche, not that I would've known what to call it then. At the time I was a lot flustered and not a little intrigued by the flattering attention of this handsome older man in the museum.

I remember his clothes quite vividly, for some reason, though I don't often notice such things now. Over a blue denim work shirt he wore a soft chamois leather hunting jacket with great big scoop-shaped pockets, dark green trousers, and a braided leather belt. He carried a small knapsack, but I remember his jacket best. I can smell it still, in my memory. (Why is it that we have phrases like "the mind's eye" but not "the mind's nose" or "the mind's ear"? Such a stupid omission:

More of my sensual memories are sounds and smells than sights.) His jacket smelled of Gauloises and leather and whatever the slightly grassy cologne he wore was, with an undercurrent of his skin, his sweat. If I smelled him again, I would know him instantly.

We'd gone to lunch, and then we spent the afternoon walking through the city, looking at churches, shops, galleries, alternately shy and gushing, trying to maneuver conversation without really having any single language in common. I didn't speak much French, he didn't speak much English and he seemed shaky in German, or at any rate uncomfortable. We eventually taught one another fairly well, a phrase here, a phrase there, much of it in bed. I learned French in the Horizontal School of Gallic Studies.

His name was Paul. I remember that. He told me his family name once, but I, never one to remember names, have to confess that I forgot it quite a while ago. Does that make me a tramp, not knowing the last name of the man who took my virginity? It can hardly matter now, I suppose. It isn't as important as the fact that we kissed for the first time in the doorway of a church, ducking in out of a rain shower, or that I can still remember how it felt to have the hot red flush of half-embarrassed arousal spreading over my cheeks and down my neck when he reached across the dinner table and caressed the side of my face.

I was so scared by it all, trembly and with no idea what was going to happen, but light-headedly high on the exhilaration. He kissed me shortly after we left the restaurant where we'd eaten supper, a for-real kiss, a kiss that left me literally breathless, holding on to his shoulders with both hands and shaking. I was eighteen, and though it sounds unbearably young to me now—if I had an eighteen-year-old daughter I certainly wouldn't want her doing what I was doing at eighteen, but I suspect that most mothers feel that way—I think in retrospect that it was the perfect age for me to have been introduced to the erotic.

I never told him that I was a virgin. I was too proud, I suppose, or else too afraid to admit I didn't really know what I was doing. I lied about my age, told him I was twenty-one, and I remember so clearly the way he held me then, the way his hand tightened around my upper arm when he kissed me, and his other hand flattened between my shoulder blades, his fingers fanning out, supporting me, strong, pulling me to him with an extraordinary guttural sigh.

It's never like that again, never quite the same. The first time, when it's all so shatteringly new, everything is so scaldingly vivid, searing you like a flare whose afterimage you see long afterward on the backs of your eyelids. Yes, of course, it is delicious later. Exquisite, even, with its own delights and pleasures that a first time can't hope to match. But still, that first time is something unto itself. Sometimes I wish I could have just one more first time, now that I know what to do with it.

But I digress.

He offered to walk me back to my hostel, and we walked along in tense erotic silence, the almost-embarrassed stillness that comes after the first physical confession of desire and before one knows how, or really whether, that confession will be received. What a scholar of minutiae one becomes in those moments when every gesture is analyzed, every word, every breath is feverishly turned over for significance, weighed for its density, judged.

I was shivering in my light skirt and sweater, my teeth chattering. He gently lifted my backpack off my shoulders and draped his jacket over them, carrying my bag for me as we walked on in the beginnings of a cold drizzle. When we reached the hostel I turned to him, not sure how to say goodnight or thank you, not sure I wanted to leave and go inside, not sure whether I dared imagine anything else.

I gave him back his jacket as we stood at the hostel door, feeling somehow more lost when I lifted its reassuring weight off my shoulders. I embraced him as he put it back on, sliding my arms between his back and the lining of the jacket, still warm with the heat of my body. I have never been able to embrace anyone like that since—slipping my arms between a person and their coat, huddling into that deliciously intimate orbit of body warmth—without having that person turn (if only for a second and only in my mind) into my first lover. I remember pressing close to him, operating on instinct, the length of my body against him, and I remember the urgent gratitude of his arms enfolding me, his voice whispering something incomprehensible into my hair as he clasped me closer still. Somehow it was clear to me then that I wasn't going to spend the night in the youth hostel at all.

The bed in his room upstairs at the small *gasthaus* creaked. It rocked a little too, the joints obviously well-worn and perhaps no longer as strong as they had once been, maternally cradling us while we rocked into one another under the thin duvets, on the starched, darned sheets. I remember bright, shocking instants of that night: Technicolor glimpses of ass and thigh, hair and belly, more than half a life ago and almost fresh enough to smell.

I remember his hands knotting in the hair at the nape of my neck, pulling my head back, my neck stretching and arching backward for his hungry kisses, his teeth sharp on my skin but careful not to hurt. Moaning softly, unthinking, I was shocked and tremendously aroused when he pulled my head back like that, shocked by my own noise and the lava blossom between my thighs that threatened to burst when he held my head that way, pulling my hair just enough to show me.

Why did I just write "show me"? Show me what? Show me that he wanted me, I suppose, or perhaps show me that I was his now, that he was taking what he desired? Show me that I was desired, show me that he knew how to make my body arch and sing with sensation and need? Show me, on some level, how to acquiesce, how to yield while at the same time making my own insistent demands? Yes, all those things and probably more as well, things it took me many more lovers to learn thoroughly, things I only now seem to have the latitude and perspective to begin to articulate. But he began, at any rate, to show me.

I remember how his hands felt against my sides when he started to push my sweater up, over my belly, uncovering my breasts. We didn't speak except for soft murmurs, encouraging noises, sounds of pleasure and surprise. He had long fingers, I recall, and they were smooth as they brushed my sides, grazing over my teen-pudge tummy and the elastic band of my bra. Eager to seem like I knew what I was doing, I raised my arms and he pulled my sweater over my head, dropping it on the floor.

His eyes widened and he looked at me in my blue skirt and prim white bra. The bra embarrassed me, ugly white cotton with a stupid little ribbon bow between the cups, a bra my mother had bought me. I whipped it off, ashamed of it, and pitched it into the corner, where it remained when we left the hotel together a day or so later.

We stood between the bureau and the bed, kissing ferociously, nipping and purring, undressing one another: his shirt, my skirt, his shoes and socks, my tights. I remember gasping out loud and shivering hard enough to make him chuckle and stroke my back the first time my breasts pressed his bare chest, our bellies touching, the sleek warmth of his skin against mine. Shortly thereafter I ventured to touch his cock, and that was another thing again. I had felt erections before, prodding me insistently in the hip or belly as I kissed a high school boyfriend, but I hadn't touched one. To be honest, I hadn't really wanted to until then, but things change.

I was bold for a virgin, I think. I stepped back from him slightly and unbuckled his belt. He smiled, stroked my hands with his, then put his hands on my shoulders and watched my hands as I unfastened his trousers, slid the zipper down its track. I looked at him as if asking his permission, flattening my hand against his belly just above the waistband of his underwear. He wore blue briefs, bikini-cut, and it seemed almost as if his cock were trying to tear them off, pressing so hard into the waistband and against the fabric that I was astonished. The muscles of his belly tensed, and he nodded, his eyes meeting mine with a look I still don't know how to characterize—perhaps he was as panicked, and as eager, as I.

The next instant I had encircled his shaft with my fingers, unsure what to do, what to say, intensely aroused by the feel of the alien creature in my hand, perhaps somewhat afraid of its amplitude, its rigidity, definitely somewhat seduced already by the impossibly fine satin of the taut-skinned cylinder. He moaned, leaning into me, burrowing his face into the crook of my neck, one arm around my shoulders, the other hand sliding from my shoulder to my breast, covering and cupping it in the basket of his fingers.

I'm not sure how I knew what to do, how to move and touch. All I remember is trying to listen to his gasps, his bass-growl moaning, his strained, breathy mutters. I wanted more of that, and kept doing whatever made him moan and whisper, basking with unrestrained delight in the sable-furred flow of his dark, basso purr. With the vibrations of his moans against my neck, then against my lips as our mouths met again, with every press of his body against mine, I smoldered hotter. I fought my moans for a little while, worried they would be somehow unseemly. But I also know I cried out in spite of myself when his head descended to my breast and his lips found my nipple, because I remember how loud it seemed in my own ears. I remember that, and I remember the way his cock thickened and throbbed in my hand at the sound.

His cock was large. Not monstrous, but big. I suppose anything would've seemed big to me at that point, given my lack of anything to compare it to, but I remember it in my hand so well that I have been able to compare it, albeit retrospectively. Longer than my hand from the heel of my palm to the tip of my middle finger, by an inch, perhaps, and thick enough that I could just touch my thumb and index finger around his shaft as I stroked it. It seemed formidable. I remember thinking to myself quite clearly, succinctly, *I know that technically it's supposed to go in there, but I can't imagine how it'll fit.* I didn't think about it in terms of pain. I wasn't afraid of it so much as I simply couldn't fathom it happening.

It did hurt some, when he began to enter me. I was wet, soakingly so. He had slipped his fingers into me with great delight, cooing delightedly at the juices that had already begun to mat my pubic hair by the time he had me out of my skirt and panties and lying back on the bed, one of his arms under me holding me to him, the other hand stroking my thighs, my mound, parting the puffy, swollen lips of my pussy. The touches of his fingers were extraordinary, shimmering and electric, gleaming bolts of sensation making me sigh and arch into his hand, clinging with my arms around his shoulders. I remember kissing him feverishly, unable to get enough of his lips on mine and the density and weight of his body against me. It was more than new, and more than terrifying, and still I was so unbearably aroused by him, by the situation, by the seduction, by the knowledge of what was about to happen (oh, all the whispered gossip at the cafeteria lunch table when we saw Tiffany Chamberlain, our high school's "town pump," passing by with her latest boyfriend! Oh, the pilfered copy of *The Joy of Sex* that my friend Andrea and I used to point at, half aroused and half horrified, in her frilly suburban bedroom!), that in those bed-bound, breathless moments I couldn't imagine ever having wanted anything more.

I trusted him more than I should have. He didn't use a condom with me, not that night or during the remaining days we spent together, and I suppose I am lucky that I neither got myself knocked up nor infected with something either embarrassing or potentially fatal. This was, after all, after AIDS had made its ghastly debut, little that I thought or knew about it at that age. They say God looks out for drunks, little children and animals, and though I'm less than comfortable trying to surmise into which of those three categories God must think I fall, it often seems that He looks out for me as well.

I trusted Paul, though, and I looked into his eyes, utterly open, waiting, as he stroked up and down my pussy with the tip of his cock. I remember thinking only that yes, it was what I wanted—I wanted with such desperation to be filled, to feel him inside me. That's the sensation that has always floored me, left me gasping and watching myself, almost as if I were a bystander viewing my desire to be fucked as almost an independent force, a creature unto itself. I grew impatient when he kept teasing my clit with the head of his cock, slipsliding through my wetness, no doubt trying to tease me close to orgasm before pushing inside. I remember instinctively pressing my hips toward him, my ass lifting up off the bed, my thighs clasping his hips. I wonder whether I winced when he pushed inside my cunt. It did hurt, a little, a thick, marrow-deep sensation of something yielding, perhaps tearing a bit, inside me.

I can remember that sensation vividly, and I have remembered it often since then when other lovers have entered me. As profound as prayer, and much the same, opening myself and inviting something into me, being blessed to have it be something so precisely right. It's the yielding, the letting-in, not so much giving something up as reclaiming something, some barrier I no longer want or need finally being broken. I want to be filled. Do I dare say that it's a desire to be completed, in some primal, unspeakable way? I may as well be honest and say it is; when my arousal takes me to that point, being penetrated completes the circuitry of my psyche and my agitated nerves, and finally I can abandon myself and be ecstatically lost in the repetition and sensation of being fucked. No, I don't have to be fucked to come, but I do have to be fucked to be released into the place where I no longer know who I am, and I no longer care that I don't know.

I wonder where he is now, my Frenchman, the one who taught me what it was like to be loved that way. I wonder whether he is still alive or whether he has died. I wonder if, when he left me, several days and a few cities later, he went back to France and to a wife, a family. Did he ever wonder if he might have had a child by me? Might he have felt guilty for leaving me, eighteen years old and collapsing with loss, my cunt freshly full of his ecstasy from our last—not that I knew it was the last—wild-eyed fuck in the tiny train bathroom, an hour before he got off the train in Braunschweig and left me on board, bound for Hanover? I will never know.

I smelled of his body for days afterward. I was so saturated with him and his juices that he was embedded in my body, physically pene-trating me long after he left, stinging olfactory reminders of him liter-ally embedded in my body, where I could not escape them. We had fucked each other hard and long, again and again, and every time I smelled him on me, in me, it reminded me who he was.

He was an opportunist. Maybe he was a bastard too. Still, Paul taught me more than I realized then. From him, I learned how to take insane sweet plunges, how to say "I love you" with a heart full enough of passion that there's not much room for regret. It's a good thing; there hasn't been much space in my life for second guesses.

He fed me blood oranges and bittersweet chocolate in bed. He licked his own come from my cunt, driving his tongue into my pussy to hear me gasp and sigh, suckling my clit between his lips as if it were my nipple and he my nursing baby. He kissed me with our juices mixed on his lips, on his tongue. We listened to the radiator pipes clanking and we laughed at our dishevelment, our sweat-matted hair and the stains on the sheets and the dried white on our bellies and thighs, until suddenly we were doing it again, me on top of him, his hands holding my hips as I moved against him with his cock buried deep inside my body, crazy-drunk on the joy of it.

We fucked literally all night that first night, his fingers stroking in and out of me when his cock couldn't, his lips and tongue teaching me that I had many different shades of climax; his arms around me, tender and sheltering, when I lay there, so drained and raw from repeated climax that when he forced one more orgasm out of me I just wept. He held me, sweet and silent and strong, until it passed, and as it passed, he stroked me slowly and deliberately to orgasm again with his fingers and told me he loved me.

Did I believe him when he said he loved me? Of course I did. I believed him and never once thought beyond it, didn't think about the future or all the romantic claptrap I might have expected from myself at that age. I was too overwhelmed, too busy just trying to react to the newness of it all and the strange sacredness of reciprocated lust. As far as I was capable, I loved him, too.

The sun came up on us still going at it, his fingers lightly flickering over my clit as he bent me over the edge of the bed and slowly, slowly-with Nivea cream as lube, the thick white kind that comes in a squat round tin—working his cock into my asshole with such gentle persistence that I cannot remember a single instant of pain, only a deep, if unfamiliar pleasure. By the time we slept that morning, we had fucked in every way we could have. He oozed from my pussy and ass, and I could still taste the slightly bitter saltiness that lingered in my mouth as I drifted off to sleep curled in his arms. I remember waking up, slightly sore, and stretching alongside his still-sleeping body, thinking smugly, *Well, I certainly did a thorough job of that.*

He and I stayed together for a week, traveling, fucking, loving, until one day he said he had to go home and told me goodbye. No phone number, no address, no lingering adieu. I cried, of course. God, how I cried, bereft the way I think only a teenager can be. For the first and last time in my life, I cried over a lover and cried him completely out in one fell swoop.

When I finally stopped crying I felt strangely serene, somehow satisfied, just as I did the morning after he took my virginity. I loved him, he left, I suffered, and it was done. There's a certain pristine quality to that kind of love affair—cause and effect clearly delineated, neatly defined, devoid of all the messy strings of breaking the news to your friends and deciding who keeps the couch—that I instinctively find satisfying. If there was a lesson in my relationship with Paul, I think it was the lesson of how to go to the end of my strength, to the point of collapse and tears, and go on. He was, after all is said and done, only the first, and there are many debts one can only repay by passing them on to someone else.

Jessica Melusine

SPARK ME

The Midwest was golden that time of year—gold grain, gold fields, crisp oranges, reds, yellows; the antiqued orange paint that marked the train. When it rattled and vibrated its way along the south shore of Lake Michigan, I thought of her hands and my lips, and moaned softly so it fit between the noise of grinding metal.

It was like this: I would stride up Michigan Avenue, far away from graduate school, my black skirt and leather jacket and broad-brimmed velvet hat not such an oddity there. I'd wait for the bus and feel my thighs grow wet, my heart pound, my body electrify. My hand would reach into my pocket and crumple the printout of her last email. I would light a Camel and think about her holding her cigarette out to my Zippo. *Spark me, baby,* she'd say.

What that meant was that I'd have my face buried between her thighs, tonguing her until she howled and sank her fingers into my black-dyed hair, smearing me with her. Of course, this would be after the club and cheap 4 a.m. breakfasts and greasy sausage and too many free drinks. *Spark me, baby. Spark me.* And that's what I would think of through the bus ride and the El and the five-block walk to the ramshackle apartment above the Chinese herbalist, where the bedroom walls smelled like ginger and licorice and five-spice powder. There she was and her lips would be on mine. My hat would fall to the floor and

I wouldn't care because of her tongue in my mouth. She'd break away and hug me tightly and I would whisper into her long violet hair, It's so good to see you again.

Sometimes we would make it to the bedroom and sometimes we would fall onto the futon in the cramped and so small living room, where the skeleton lights watched, a string of rattling voyeurs. I lifted her faded black cotton Current 93 shirt above her breasts so I could lick and kiss along her belly, work my way up to her nipples and full, heavy, sweet round breasts. My lips spiraled around them as she arched and moaned, rocking her hips up to shed the black broomstick skirt, showing the purple and black tights she cut down to stockings, the Frederick's garter belt, the full, sweet swelling of her thighs and belly, the voluptuous splendor of her ass. I made love with my boots on, all fishnet and silver rings and bare flesh as I kissed and kissed and felt her eyes open in dark blue splendor even though I couldn't see as I licked round each nipple, then slowly down to her navel and moved my tongue between her thighs, tracing her clit. I sucked as the walls rattled from the El and the Psychedelic Furs CD, and her cries were sweeter and more heartbreaking than any of Richard Butler's words.

My face wet and glistening, she worked her fingers in me, quick and sweet, rubbing, her hair a lilac silk curtain on my skin and her lips just like, just like heaven. And with four of her fingers in me I would come, crying and gasping, knowing the neighbors would hear and not caring. After that, we shared a cigarette—*smooth as a milkshake*, she'd say— and I'd watch the smoke curl from her pink lips as if I could use it to read the future. Of course I could—it was far away on Sunday, and hours of classes and nights away from her soft skin. *Love what we have, dear*, she said, but she knew it, too.

We danced at night or sat and smoked around the red barbecue candles at Onyx, made our fingers bob up and down in time to KMFDM and the Sisters. She bummed drinks from the bartender and I paid for cabs. Sometimes when we were drunk, we would babble about theory, Kristeva and Califia and Eris Discordia, and my fingers would find hers and we would be home fast fast fast and we would be upstairs, my fingers in her, fucking, her face below me shiny with glammy makeup and thick dark eyeliner. When we awoke, we were covered in lipstick and gleaming from glitter. And our eyes looked like we had been crying, smeared with black.

We hung out, her, me, a posse of black-clad friends, shopping on Belmont. But all I remember of that fall is her, eyes dark blue behind the shiny lenses of her glasses, hair in electric lavender braids, leather jacket, pink Little Twin Stars backpack, mother-goddess curves of hip and ass pushing out her black skirt under the tight waist of her biker jacket. I looked so I would remember, and I know I kissed her as the air turned colder and I turned closer to going away.

We were harder and faster in those days before November. We would make love on the bed and she would bite down on the pillows as I worked one-two-three-four-five fingers into her. My latex glove squeaked at her every wiggle and all was her hot, heavy scent. Her skin and mine prickled at the cold drafts that came around the windows. And as she cried, and I felt her deep blood-pulsing heat around my hand, I would howl and scratch my nails down her back until she convulsed, wet and shuddering around me.

When her hand was in me, her breasts and hard nipples and silky skin against my back and her hair a purple cloud around me, I cried out and opened up for her, wanting the days to move as slowly as her motions inside my cunt. But the days came as fast as my orgasm and faster than sleep in her arms.

It was on my last trip that I cried the whole way to Chicago. The difference: She met me at the train station and we clenched hands on the bus, black-gloved fingers in an almost unbreakable knot. She opened the door to the apartment and she was the one that pushed me to the bed, tearing the buttons from my black velvet shirt, stripping me of thermal tights, boots, black lace skirt. Outside the window the temperature dropped and the sky turned to the black of evening—black as our leathers, our skirts and our army boots, the color that veiled us and made us shine like stars against it. Inside, I burned like a candle flame. With tears in her eyes she kissed me, her tongue tracing runes and ritual marks on my skin. I shivered and moaned as my blood turned to gold.

Her lips bred lightning, her fingers flicked and pinched at my nipples, teasing the barbells, as if she would only remember my body by touch. Her tongue bathed me everywhere, tracing each lip, looping around my ear, thighs, the curve between ass and thigh, my clit, my fingers—and then she kissed me, full, long and sweet. We were fire, incandescence in the heavy Midwestern darkness, and when her hand penetrated me, fucking me hard and heavy as tears ran down her face, I screamed in pleasure and squeezed her so tight I thought I could hold her inside me forever. We held each other, bodies slick and heavy as night came on.

When the dawn came, I left. I had to—there was a fellowship, a PhD program. Too far away. There were letters, emails—I sent her a pocket-knife shaped like a crucifix and chocolate eyeballs for Christmas—and then we fell away like autumn leaves, spinning into darkness.

But I can't help it. Someday I will go back, and ride the same train. In my mind, it will be edged with rust. Someone else lives in the sweet-spiced apartment, but I can't help that either. Perhaps I will walk into Onyx and against all reason she will be there and her hair will glow luminous violet in the candle flames and the DJ will play "Some Kind of Stranger." Her black-lined eyes will shine blue and perhaps edge with tears behind her glasses. And she will open her *Labyrinth* lunchbox and pull out a cigarette. She'll smile and I will melt between my heart and thighs. *Spark me, baby. Spark me.*

Zonna

Stone Cold *(A Confession)*

I could have been kinder. She loved me, after all—whatever those words might have meant to her. Even if I didn't believe it. Even if it didn't make sense. Even if I thought she was mistaken. Love and lust are kissing cousins. You know you can, technically, but you know you shouldn't. You're crossing a barrier, a line.

She was straight. I'm sure of it. She wasn't bisexual. She wasn't just finding her way out. She wasn't looking to experiment. She didn't stare at other women and wonder *what if*. She wanted me. To be with me. To kiss *me*. My tongue teasing her, my fingers stroking her, my fist filling her up until she couldn't breathe.

Why was she so attracted to me? I don't know. Maybe because I looked like a boy. Maybe because I acted more like a boy than the boys she knew. Maybe it was the way I smelled, or my crooked smile, or the muscles in my arms. My boots, my hair, my voice? It could have been any of those things, or maybe it was something else altogether. Or not. Maybe it was nothing in particular.

At first, I told her no. No way. Not interested. It would be messy and pointless, and I didn't exist just to satisfy her curiosity, if that's what it was. Her husband, colorless as he might have seemed, actually owned a gun. Why would I want to go that route? But she persisted: writing me scalding email; calling me three, even four times a day; showing up where she knew I'd be and then just waiting. She wouldn't interrupt me if I was talking to my friends at the bar; she'd just sit a few stools away so I'd know she was there, available. And when I left, she'd follow me to the parking lot, silently wondering if this would be the night I'd scoop her up and take her with me.

It was tempting to know how much she wanted me, flattering, empowering. I didn't imagine I'd change her into something she wasn't or could never be. I didn't expect her to leave her husband or her two scroungy dogs and jump on the back of my bike and ride into the blazing sunset. I honestly didn't even like her all that much. But I did know I'd leave a mark, however small or indiscernible. I'd know, and she'd know.

Who doesn't want to be the first—a pioneer, blazing a trail that others, at their very best, could only follow? She was a virgin peak that only I could scale. I imagined reaching the top and peering down at everyone else like they were so many tiny black ants. It was a pleasant image.

But where was the challenge? Surrender is not a true victory. What could I fight for? What could I conquer? I gave myself headaches, devising complicated strategies and then abandoning them. The answer was so simple, I almost thought right past it. We both knew how willing she was to give herself to me. I would take something from her, instead. It was such a perfect, subtle distinction, like the difference between "yes" and "please."

The first time . . . I've never in my whole life seen anyone who wanted it so badly. I kissed her and she dissolved into a puddle. Her olive-brown skin was hot on my fingers; it sizzled everywhere I touched her. She stripped for me, her dark eyes never leaving my face. Her hands shook as she revealed herself inch by inch: plump, round breasts with magenta nipples; chubby thighs, the kind you want to bite. I made her lay there, naked, on the bed and wait until I was good and ready, wait just a few beats past too long, until I saw the doubt cloud her wondering eyes.

I could have strapped one on, but I didn't want to do her that way.

It would have been too easy. I had to find something she couldn't compare to anything else she'd ever done. Something she'd remember.

I teased her by alternately sucking her nipples softly, then pinching them hard until she cried out. I watched worry crease her brow. Would I hurt her? She had no way of knowing how far she could trust me. Still, she let me do what I liked, and after a while it was clear how aroused she was.

When I sensed she was ready for more, I whispered what I planned to do, hot breath in her ear. "I'm gonna fuck you now, like you've never been fucked before." Her pussy started to glisten as I said the words. "I'm gonna put my fist inside you and fuck you hard."

I grabbed a generous amount of lube and eased two fingers inside her, pleased to find how wet she was already. She spread her legs wider for me, sighing as I explored further. Three fingers made her groan. Four made her gasp, and I waited for her to adjust before folding my thumb and sliding all the way in.

She was moaning and sweating and rubbing her own dusky nipples in a way that really turned me on. When she started humping my hand, I knew it was time. I didn't even take my jacket off. I knew the feel of my sleeve rubbing up against her clit as I pumped my fist slowly in and out of her cunt was driving her crazy. The smell of leather and sweat and her mixed together; I breathed it in, intoxicated. She whimpered, then moaned, a deep-throated tone that came from somewhere primal. She seemed to take it all right as I pounded deeper and deeper into her with each thrust.

The sounds that came from the back of her throat made me want to fuck her harder. By the time she came I was grunting along with her, short guttural sounds, in a voice I barely recognized as my own. After, I let her rest her head on my shoulder while she caught her breath. She didn't cry. I remember thinking she would. I think I was disappointed.

But that's not what the story's about. It's about what came later. I'd seen her a few times by then. She'd become curious about touching me. I'd moved her hands away in each instance, telling her it wasn't something that was going to happen. I explained my boundaries to her, but I knew she didn't understand. How could she? The entire experience had been strange to begin with, and now I was asking her to wrap her brain around a concept so foreign to her I may as well have been speaking another language. So she continued to try, and I continued to dissuade her.

And then one night the impossible happened. I changed my mind.

Her soft hands slid under my T-shirt and I let them. I felt her nails scratch across my nipples. Her fingers fumbled clumsily with my zipper and I did nothing to stop them. I even allowed her to slip my jeans down. I wanted her to touch me. What was I thinking? I wasn't. Wasn't thinking. I was delirious with a fever I'd never had before.

She slipped her hand inside my boxers to find my hot cunt waiting for her. She moved her fingers around, searching for my clit and sending a shock right through me when she found it. I lifted my hips to encourage her. I spread my legs as wide as I could with my jeans still around my knees, willing her to rub harder. It was beginning to feel really good. And suddenly she stopped, her hands disappeared. I opened my eyes. She was crying.

"I can't," she said. "I don't know what I'm doing."

I could've been understanding. I could've told her she was doing fine. I could've guided her hand and showed her what I needed. I could've said it was okay, that she didn't have to do anything she wasn't ready for.

Instead, I pulled my jeans back on and got out of bed. I lit a cigarette, told her to leave. I said things like "I knew I shouldn't have trusted you," and "That's what I get for messing with a straight girl." I hurled words at her, words like "tease" and "bitch."

She cried and begged me to be patient, to let her try again. She said she loved me. She was sorry. She was just scared; she felt like she was in over her head—drowning, drowning. Couldn't I teach her? Couldn't I give her another chance?

"Go back to your husband," I snarled. "Go back where you belong."

It was the meanest thing I could think of. It crushed her. That was the desired effect.

Like I said, I could have been kinder. She loved me, after all—whatever those words might have meant to her. But pride is a funny thing. It was important that I demolish hers in order to save my own. She ran away feeling like a loser, a complete failure. I'd been the first, and I'd left her with a permanent limp.

If she only knew she'd been the first as well.

Helena Settimana

When We Were One

In the fall of 1978, our first year, we all came to live together in a walk-up flat overlooking the busy, smelly streets of Toronto's Kensington Market. The flat smelled like curry. Once-filled synagogues, old Hebrew chicken vendors, screaming Portuguese goat-sellers, Chinese grocers spilling their wares into the narrow streets and Indian spice merchants reeking of cardamom and cumin—all these were our neighbors. Agnes, Leo, Wulf and I shared the space while we tried to make it through art school.

We were going to live forever, conquer the world, be the next Warhol, exist on the edge, love forever, leave beautiful corpses. It was so facile, so easy, so natural. We were all one. Who would question the opportunity to immerse oneself in love, in lust, in the smoke and the juice and the sweetberry wine of a nest packed tight with lovers? We were confident that the experiments of the preceding decade and the excesses of the early seventies provided the perfect canvas for the lives of four creative souls floating in the yellow haze of honey-oil smoke, amber and patchouli in the acid-blue night air.

We drank espresso and smoked Gitanes and Gauloises. We dressed in black, mostly, except Agnes, who looked like Ariel from *The Tempest* might have—all gauzy and fluttery as a fairy dressed in dragonfly's wings. We hated disco, loved Zappa, Zep, Ziggy; wondered what we really felt about the Sex Pistols. We were too young to be hippies, too old to be yuppies. We were artists, and for each the breath of the next was essential for the existence of us all. There was no name for us.

We fucked in a pack.

Wulf looked like an exotic Heathcliff—you know, the brooding, lantern-jawed hero of *Wuthering Heights*. His mum was English, his dad, sort-of-African from Trinidad. Wulf was all cinnamon and jet and Persian-lamb curls. His mum had named him Beowulf in a thoughtless gesture of intellectual patriotism. He favored ankle-length greatcoats, black jeans, army-surplus sweaters that made him seem even larger than his six-foot frame, army boots from England, Che Guevara T-shirts. He painted big splashy canvases so full of color they more than compensated for his own somber exterior.

Agnes was frail and delicate, with pale blonde hair and skim-milk-white skin through which her veins shone blue. Her thighs were laced with cobwebby blotches of pink and violet. She painted big pictures, too, with lines of her poetry scratched through wet oil to emerge, as spectral as the woman who made them, like something half remembered or half realized, something subliminal. Hot. Her words were hot like the newly forged edge of a blade. They entered you by degrees, like an insidious disease and tore a pathway to your balls, your cunt, your heart. That was the thrill of Agnes. She was subversive.

Leo made prints. Leo's lithographs were like a guided tour of the underworld. He said they were a tribute to his grandfather's memories of the Holocaust. Leo's coiled Mediterranean hair twisted into tiny nubs, baby dreads. He had eyes the color of the bottom of some swimming pool. Leo wore leather and chains and black eyeliner when it suited. He made us consider the Sex Pistols. He had good weed. He had microdot. He had Temple Ball. Leo was packing nirvana and a ten-inch stump to boot. He was also funny and sweet. Go figure.

And me. I took photographs and developed the film. I was the archivist, the documentarian and the center that held our loosely kept secret for nearly twenty years.

When the call came from the television studio inquiring about pictures

I had of our "group marriage," as the researcher called it, all those memories flooded back. They wanted to do a story about "alternative lifestyles of the seventies," and rumors of four young artists and their faithful record of their love had reached the right people. I pulled the prints from the storeroom, lit some patchouli, filled my bowl and allowed myself to feel the passion, the purpose, the camaraderie of a time when we were more than family. When we were one.

It started when I came back early from the college darkroom, kicking through the rustling piles of maple leaves carpeting the sidewalks. I was hoping to catch Wulf at home painting in his room—to see him alone. The apartment was hazy with the smoke and smell of pot and exotic perfume. The frantic strains of David Bowie spitting out "Suffragette City" rolled from the half-opened door of Wulf's room.

I couldn't see Wulf, but I could see Agnes, her head thrown back, blonde hair floating in a wide arc and one tiny, upturned breast bouncing in an erratic circle. She was smeared in paint, panting. Pagan. I should have known they would find each other irresistible. The breast was covered by a brown hand like a shadow cast across the face of the moon. I took a step back.

"AAAAAAAhhhhh . . . wham, bam, thank you ma'am!"

When Wulf's hand squeezed, Agnes's eyes flew open and she saw me. She saw me and she laughed, but it was the sweetest laugh—tinkling fairy bells. Somehow, that registered through my shock. That, and the fact that she was so damned beautiful in that moment. It stopped me. It almost got me out of the way of my embarrassment, made my heart start beating again. She slowly toppled backward, and the next thing I knew, Wulf was coming through the door, his fading erection wagging before him. Jesus, I couldn't help but stare. He was smeared with paint, too, like some kind of mad warrior king.

I turned and fled to the kitchen, calling over my shoulder. "Oh-my-god-you-two-I-am-so-sorry-that-I-just-walked-in-like-that-oh-my-god-I-am-so-embarrassed-I-can't-believe-I-did-that-oh-I . . ."

I sat, allowing the hammering of my heart to subside, and discovered that the pulse lingered between my legs, drumming. I figured they'd go back and shut the door and continue, but Wulf came into the kitchen bearing a joint and a glass of good red plonk, and handed me both, telling me he thought I might need some help to work the shock out. I couldn't look at him. I wasn't angry. I wasn't hurt, either, although I thought that I should be. It would be the decent thing to do. His hand rested lightly on my shoulder, a warm and comforting thing, very strange under the circumstances.

He said, "We wondered if you were coming home early, but you know, we got into the smoke and then one thing led to another and the next, well . . ." he trailed off, shrugging. "Do you want to see what we were doing?" I looked at him wide-eyed. "I was painting, Bee, I was painting. Painting Agnes. Have a toke and come look."

"I thought you were fucking Agnes . . ." I said with a tinge of wonder in my voice.

"Yeah, well, that too . . . come on, come look."

Agnes still lay curled on the mattress in the corner of his room, smeared gaudily and wound in the Indian cotton tablecloths that passed for sheets and wrappers in Wulf's little world. She smiled giddily up at me, her eyes a little over-bright. He turned the easel to face me. Agnes's image spread itself across the canvas, her vulva swollen and prominent, her hips raised, the underside of her breasts and her chin visible, fading away with the perspective. The painting was hot. I could slip my hand inside there and be swallowed up if I just closed my eyes and imagined it.

"Jesus, Wulf, where are you gonna hang that thing?" I asked. Agnes's pussy was painted in reds and hot pinks and purples. You could smell the color over the faint ammoniac odor of the acrylics he used.

Agnes stirred from her corner of the room. "I'm going to put on some more music. what do you want?"

"Don't care," I replied, feeling buzzed all of a sudden. Then I changed my mind. "How about *Minstrel in the Gallery?* That feels about right for the present situation." I started to giggle. "I really am sorry you guys, I mean, I had no idea."

Agnes whirled back into the bedroom, singing in her piping voice along with Ian Anderson's growl. "Yeah, bad timing, Bee . . . and I am still so horny . . ." She looked at Wulf. Wulf looked at me. I held my smoke and felt my knees buckle and the ceiling above my head crack open. Cerulean blue all around.

"Do you want to stay, Bee, or do you wanna, um, go? I don't mind. Actually, I'd like you to stay. So would Agnes."

She nodded and added thickly, "Yeah, that would be so hot."

Yeah, that would be so hot . . . My legs began to sag like wet tissue. "I feel a bit woozy," I said. Wulf suggested I lie down on his pile of a bed and take a load off. I don't know how my clothes came off.

So I slid onto that pallet and watched while the ceiling whirled and tilted crazily and the music bore me through the heavy air to hover like a succubus over Wulf and Agnes, who made their own art in dark and light beside his easel and the old wooden chair. They seemed to move in slow motion. I watched from the corner of the ceiling until the weight between my legs pulled me back. I found myself aware of the bed once again, the camera poking into my side. I slowly pulled it out, fiddled with the focus and the f-stop, and called, "Hey, guys," and depressed the shutter. The camera whirred as it advanced. I pressed it again. Agnes moaned like she was dying. They were fucking standing up, and he turned her so that she could bend backward and make an artful arc for me to capture. She was gabbling giddily, her legs bobbing and criss-crossing around his high, muscular ass. God, they were beautiful. He staggered wide-legged and stood over me. The camera whined.

Agnes was keening her need: high, crystalline. "Fu-uck meeee." Wulf let her down beside me, pushed her head into the pillows so that her ass waved in the air, luminescent, purple at its core. I stood unsteadily, aiming my camera at where he joined himself to her; at her face, absorbed, open; at the streaks of color slashed across their bodies. That was the time I took that photograph over there. That moment.

He grabbed my wrist hard and pulled me off balance so that I knelt beside him, and he kissed my face, bit my lips and drew me seamlessly into them so there was no longer any distance, any resistance. His skin expanded to accommodate my presence. Just one. One plus one plus one equals one.

Agnes came. Agnes came so hard I imagined the chicken sellers on the street trying to placate their caged, startled stock; the goats hidden in back rooms bleating in fear. Her cry became the center of the room, of us. It filled everything. It brought me dangerously, deliciously close to the edge.

It was about then that we became aware of Leo standing in the doorway with a dumb expression on his face, his mouth a tiny *o*. I have the picture to prove it. Wulf pulled out and Agnes rolled away, spent, crumpling against the wall, and looked at him. Wulf's shiny brown dick pointed at Leo, grazed my cheek. Sweat, linen, seawater, amber—the smell was overwhelming. Breathy flute sounds soared from the stereo.

"You gonna stand there, or are you gonna join the party?"

"Yeah, Leo, come join the party," sang Agnes, looking half asleep.

Anderson was droning in his nasal, coronet voice about some big bottle Fraulein and the Pig-Me and the Whore. I wanted Wulf. I wanted him bad. Actually I wanted them all, but I wanted to feel the prickle of the tiny pips of hair on Wulf's belly, the heavy head of his cock that looked like glazed caramel, still slick with Agnes. I caught him as he swung back in my direction. There was a sweetness to her taste, her scent which lingered down to the mat of curls in Wulf's lap.

"Man," breathed Leo, hopping from foot to foot as he struggled out of his jeans. "*Man . . .*"

He took my camera and shot some more pictures: Wulf and me, Agnes.

He wore these multicolored nylon bikini briefs. His cock strained at the waistband. Freed, it swung aggressively back at Wulf, darkening. Then he turned it on me.

Wulf stared. "Man, you are gonna give me a bad name with that thing." He laughed. "You had better keep it within the family if you don't wanna ruin my reputation."

The three of us fused, with Agnes hovering, stroking and whispering

searing little obscenities in her siren's voice, hands dancing like butterflies on our tumbling bodies. Leo and Wulf jousted cocks. Leo's ink-
stained fingers disappeared into Agnes, into me. They closed around
Wulf's meat and made the look on his face change. We were beautiful,
immortal, and we knew it with absolute certainty. I remember best the
feel and the smell when at last we all moved together. Our skins felt like
velvet riding on silk: hands, mouths, teeth, tongue, cocks, cunts. One.

Wulf's big balls slapped my ass and it felt like an embrace—warm
ripe figs being mashed into my skin. He kept telling me to open my
eyes, that he wanted me to remember, but my fuck-memory is more
tuned to smell, to taste, to feel. My camera sees for me. My body
remembers the rest. When I came, when we came, ecstatic with the
searing pain that only extreme pleasure seems to inspire, the ceiling
split again, and again and I floated off the bed, borne on buoyant
notes of violin, guitar, flute. Still, the best—the best was lying sated,
slick with the sheen of sweat and the glaze of come, the essence of all
those lovers. I can only speak for myself, but it made me feel . . .
anointed, changed and at one.

It came out in our art. Wulf's exposé of Agnes was only the start of
it. Leo's lithographs turned to life for a while: brilliant images of tumbling bodies, each absorbed in the embrace of the other, replaced the
piles of corpses he once memorialized. My pictures of us together and
alone became the focus of my attention for months. In most, I
obscured our faces, abstracting them, except for the one of Agnes
looking up at me while Wulf lost himself in her depths. That was too
beautiful to hide—that wanton innocence. Her painting, her poetry,
grew lighter, clearer. Someone wanted to record her words to music.
On graduation we held a show together. We got infamous for a time:
The Toronto Star featured the exhibit on the front of their Arts section.
We created a scandal—a sensation. We got picketed and called perverts.
We loved it, because we loved each other. One plus one plus one plus
one equals one.

But sometime in the early eighties we began to drift: Our work
pulled us to the corners of the continent. Wulf moved to New York. I

followed him briefly, but it wasn't the same without Agnes and Leo. Then Leo went to San Francisco. We called, we wrote, we whispered endearments, come-ons, lascivious daydreams. We came, screaming into our receivers, but the distance was too great and the phone bills were murder.

Agnes and I tried it on our own: It just wasn't the same without the guys. She moved to Montreal. Time had turned a page when we weren't looking. The same kismet that had brought us together in such an uncomplicated and loving way never returned. I had to stop fucking without a condom, and I mourned that milestone as if I had been robbed of something deep within myself—the passing of my elemental, molecular connection to others.

The pictures spread out before me, hauled from a box that sat in the corner of the studio storeroom for the last seventeen years. I pulled one from the pile. It was Agnes. The picture, black and white, showed her sweet face turned toward me, eyes intent on the lens, her look raw. You couldn't see Wulf in the frame, but you just knew he was there—someone was there, making her look that way.

I remember the day I took that one.

Sacchi Green

TO REMEMBER YOU BY

A movie!" she exulted from three thousand miles away. "They're making a movie of our book!"

"Our book" was *Healing Their Wings*, a bittersweet, often funny novel about American nurses in England during World War II. My grandson's wife had based it on oral histories she'd recorded from several of us who had kept in contact over the past half-century.

I rejoiced with her at the news, but then came a warning she was clearly embarrassed to have to make." The screenwriters are bound to change some things, though. There's a good chance they'll want it to be quite a bit, well, racier."

"Racier?" I asked. "Honey, all you had to do was ask the right questions!" How had she missed the passionate undertones to my story? When I spoke, all too briefly, of Cleo, had she thought the catch in my voice was merely old age taking its toll at last? The young assume that they alone have explored the wilder shores of sex; or, if not, that the flesh must inevitably forget.

I had to admit, though, that I was being unfair to her. Knowing what she did of my long, happy life with Jack, how could she even have guessed the right questions to ask? But it hardly matters now. The time is right. I'm going to share those memories, whether the movie people are ready for the truth or not. Because my flesh has never forgotten—will never forget—Cleo Remington.

In the summer of 1943, the air was sometimes so thick with sex you could have spread it like butter, and it would have melted, even on cold English toast.

The intensity of youth, the urgency of wartime, drove us. Nurses, WACs and young men hurled into the deadly air war against Germany gathered between one crisis and another in improvised dance halls. Anything from barns to airfield hangars to tents rigged from parachute silk would do. To the syncopated jive of trumpets and clarinets, to "Boogie Woogie Bugle Boy" and "Accentuate the Positive," we swayed and jitterbugged and twitched our butts defiantly at past and future. To the muted throb of drums and the yearning moan of saxophones, to "As Time Goes By" and "I'll Be Seeing You," our bodies clung and throbbed and yearned together.

I danced with men facing their mortality, and with brash young kids in denial. Either way, life pounded through their veins and bulged in their trousers, and sometimes my body responded with such force I felt as though my own skirt should have bulged with it.

But I wasn't careless. And I wasn't in love. As a nurse, I'd tried to mend too many broken boys, known too many who never made it back at all, to let my mind be clouded by love. Sometimes, though, in dark hallways or tangles of shrubbery or the shadow of a bomber's wings, I would comfort some nice young flier with my body and drive him on until his hot release geysered over my hand. Practical Application of Anatomical Theory, we nurses called it, "PAT" for short. Humor is a frail enough defense against the chaos of war, but you take what you can get.

Superstition was the other universal defense. Mine, I suppose, was a sort of vestal virgin complex, an unexamined conviction that opening my flesh to men would destroy my ability to heal theirs.

My very defenses (and repressions) might have opened me to Cleo. Would my senses have snapped so suddenly to attention in peacetime? They say war brings out things you didn't know were in you. But I think back to my first sight of her—the intense gray eyes, the thick, dark hair too short and straight for fashion, the forthright movements of her lean body—and a shiver of delight ripples through me, even now. No matter where or when we met, she would have stirred me.

The uniform sure didn't hurt, though: dark blue, tailored, with slacks instead of a skirt. I couldn't identify the service, but "USA" stood out clearly on each shoulder, so it made sense for her to be at the Red Cross Club on Charles Street in London, set up by the United States ambassador's wife for American servicewomen.

There was a real dance floor, and a good band was playing that night, but Cleo lingered near the entrance as though undecided whether to continue down the wide, curving staircase. I don't know how long I stared at her. When I looked up from puzzling over the silver pin on her breast she was watching me quizzically. My date, a former patient whose half-healed wounds made sitting out most of the dances advisable, gripped my shoulder to get my attention.

"A friend of yours?" he asked. He'd been getting a bit maudlin as they played "You'd Be So Nice To Come Home To," and I'd already decided he wasn't going to get the kind of comfort he'd been angling for. I shook off his hand.

"No," I said, "I was just trying to place the uniform. Are those really wings on her tunic?" I felt a thrill of something between envy and admiration. The high, compact breasts under the tunic had caught my attention, too, but that was more than I was ready to admit to myself. I watched her movements with more than casual interest as she descended the stairs and took a table in a dim corner.

"Yeah," he said with some bitterness, "can you believe it? They brought in women for the Air Transport Auxiliary. They get to fly everything, even the newest Spitfires, ferrying them from factories or wherever the hell else they happen to be to wherever they're needed."

His tone annoyed me, even though I knew he was anxious about whether he'd ever fly again himself. But then he pushed it too far. "I hear women are ferrying planes back in the States now, too. Thousands of 'em. Next thing you know there won't be any jobs left for men after the war. I ask you, what kind of woman would want to fly warplanes, anyway?" His smoldering glance toward the corner table told me just what kind of woman he had in mind. "Give me a cozy redheaded armful with her feet on the ground any day," he said, with a look of insistent intimacy.

"With her back on the ground, too, I suppose," I snapped, and stood up. "I'm sorry, Frank, I really do wish you the best, but I don't think there's anything more I can do for you. Maybe you should catch the early train back to the base." I evaded his grasp and retreated to the powder room; when I finally came out, he had gone. The corner table, however, was still occupied.

"Mind if I sit here?" I asked. "I'm Kay Barnes."

"Cleo Remington," she said, offering a firm handshake. "It's fine by me. Afraid the boyfriend will try again?"

So she'd noticed our little drama. "Not boyfriend," I said, "just a patient who's had all the nursing he's going to get." I signaled a waitress. "Can I get you a drink to apologize for staring when you came in? I'd never seen wings on a woman before, and . . . well, to be honest, I had a flash of insane jealousy. I've always wanted to fly, but things just never worked out that way."

"Well," Cleo said, "I can't say I've ever been jealous of a nurse's life, but I'm sure glad you're on the job."

"Tell me what being a pilot is like," I said, "so I can at least fantasize."

So she told me, over a cup of the best (and possibly only) coffee in London, about persuading her rancher father that air surveillance was the best way to keep track of cattle spread out over a large chunk of Montana. When her brother was old enough to take over the flying cowboy duty, she'd moved on to flying courier service out of Billings, and then to a job as an instructor at a Civilian Pilot Training Program in Colorado, where everyone knew that her young male students were potential military pilots, but that Cleo, in spite of all her flight hours, wasn't.

Then came all-out war, and the chance to come to England. Women aviators were being welcomed to ferry aircraft for the decimated RAF. I watched her expressive face and hands and beautifully shaped mouth as she talked of Hurricanes and Spitfires and distant glimpses of German Messerschmitts.

As she talked, I did, in fact, fantasize like crazy. But visions of moonlight over a foaming sea of clouds kept resolving into lamplight on naked skin, and the roar of engines and rush of wind gave way to pounding blood and low, urgent cries. Her shifting expressions fascinated me; her rare, flashing smile was so beautiful I wanted to feel its movement under my own lips.

I didn't know what had come over me. Or, rather, I knew just enough to sense what I wanted, without having the least idea how to tell whether she could possibly want it, too. I'd admired women before, but only aesthetically, I'd rationalized, or with mild envy; after all, I liked men just fine. But this flush of heightened sensitivity, this feeling of rushing toward some cataclysm that might tear me apart . . . this was unexplored territory.

"So," Cleo said at last, looking a bit embarrassed, "that's more about me than anybody should have to sit through. What about you? How did you end up here?"

"I'm not sure I can even remember who I was before the war," I said, scarcely knowing who I'd been just half an hour ago. "It seems as though nothing interesting or exciting ever happened to me back then. Not that 'interesting' will be a fair description of life now until I'm at a safe distance from it."

She nodded. We were silent for a while, sharing the unspoken question of whether the world would ever know such a thing as safety again. Then I told her a little about growing up in New Hampshire, and climbing mountains, only to feel that even there the sky wasn't high and wide enough to hold me. "That's when I dreamed about flying," I said.

"Yes!" she said. "I get that feeling here, once in a while, even in the air. Somehow this European sky seems smaller, and the land below is so crowded with cities, sometimes the only way to tell where you are is by the pattern of the railroads. The Iron Compass, we call it. I guess that's one reason I'm transferring back to the States instead of renewing my contract here.

"The main reason, though, is that I've heard women in the WASPs at home are getting to test-pilot huge Flying Fortresses and Marauders. And that's only the beginning. Pretty soon they'll be commissioned in the regular Army Air Forces. In Russia women are even flying combat missions; 'Night Witches,' the Germans call them. If the war goes on long enough . . . " She stopped short of saying, "If enough of our men are killed, I'll get to fight," and I was grateful. "History is being made," she went on, "and I've got to be in on it!"

In her excitement she had stretched out her legs under the table until they brushed against mine. I wanted so badly to rub against the wool of her slacks that I could scarcely pay attention to what she was saying, but I caught one vital point.

"Transferring?" I leaned far forward, and felt, as well as saw, her glance drop to my breasts. The starchy wartime diet in England had added some flesh, but at that moment I didn't mind, because all of it was tingling. "When do you go?"

"In two weeks," she said. "I'm taking a week in London to get a look at some of the sights I haven't had time to see in the whole eighteen months I've been over here. Then there'll be one more week of ferrying out of Hamble on the south coast. And then I'm leaving."

Two weeks. One, really. "I've got a few days here, too," I said. "Maybe we could see the sights together." I tried to look meaningfully into her eyes, but she looked down at her own hands on the table and then out at the dance floor where a few couples, some of them pairs of girls, were dancing.

"Sure," she said. "That would be fun." Her casual tone seemed a bit forced.

"I don't suppose you'd like to dance, would you?" I asked, with a sort of manic desperation. "Girls do it all the time here when there aren't enough men. Nobody thinks anything of it."

"They sure as hell would," Cleo said bluntly, "if they were doing it right." She met my eyes, and in the hot gray glow of her defiant gaze, I learned all I needed to know.

Then she looked away. "Not," she said carefully, "that any of Flight

Captain Jackie Cochran's handpicked cream-of-American-womanhood pilots would know anything about that."

"Of course not," I agreed. "Or any girl-next-door nurses, either." I could feel a flush rising from my neck to my face, but I plowed ahead. "Some of us might be interested in learning, though."

She looked at me with an arched eyebrow, then pushed back her chair and stood up. Before my heart could do more than lurch into my throat, she said lightly, "How about breakfast here tomorrow, and then we'll see what the big deal is about London."

It turned out we were both staying in the club dormitory upstairs. We went up two flights together; then I opened the door on the third-floor landing. Cleo's room was on the fourth floor. I paused, and she said, without too much subtlety, "One step at a time, Kay, one step at a time!" Then she bolted upward, her long legs taking the stairs two, sometimes three, steps at a time.

Instead of a return to common sense, night brought a series of dreams wilder than anything my imagination or clinical knowledge of anatomy had ever provided before. When I met Cleo for breakfast it was hard to look at her without envisioning her dark, springy hair brushing my thighs, while her mouth . . . but all my dreams had dissolved in frustration, and I had woken tangled in hot, damp sheets with my hand clamped between my legs.

Cleo didn't look all that rested, either, but for all I knew she was always like that before her second cup of coffee. When food and caffeine began to take effect, I got a map of bus routes from the porter and we planned our day.

London Bridge, Westminster Abbey, Harrods department store; whether I knew how to do it right or not, every moment was a dance of sorts. Cleo got considerable amusement out of my not-so-subtle attempts at seduction. She even egged me on to try on filmy things in Harrods that I could never afford, or have occasion to wear (what on earth, we speculated, did Harrods stock when it *wasn't* wartime?), and let me see how much she enjoyed the view. I didn't think she was just humoring me.

In the afternoon, after lunch at a quaint tearoom, we went to the British Museum and admired the cool marble flesh of nymphs and goddesses. Cleo circled a few statues, observing that the Greeks sure had a fine hand when it came to posteriors; I managed to press ever so casually back against her, and she didn't miss the chance to demonstrate her own fine hand, or seem to mind that my posterior was not quite classical.

Then we decided life was too short to waste on Egyptian mummies, and wandered a bit until, in a corner of an upper floor, we found a little gallery where paintings from the Pre-Raphaelite movement and other Victorian artists were displayed. There was no one else there but an elderly female guard whose stern face softened just a trace at Cleo's smile.

Idealized women gazed out of mythological worlds aglow with color. The grim reality of war retreated under the spell of flowing robes, rippling clouds of hair, impossibly perfect skin.

Cleo stood in the center of the room, slowly rotating. "Sure had a thing for redheads, didn't they," she said. "You'd have fit right in, Kay."

I could only hope she herself had a thing for redheads. Standing there, feeling drab in my khaki uniform, I watched Cleo appreciating the paintings of beautiful women. When she moved closer to the sleeping figure of *Flaming June* by Lord Leighton, I gazed with her at the seductive flesh gleaming through transparent orange draperies and allowed myself, experimentally, to imagine stroking the curve of thigh and hip, the round, tender breasts.

"I don't know how this rates as art," Cleo said, "but oh, my!"

A hot flush rose across my skin: Desire, yes, but also fierce jealousy. I wanted to be in that bright, serene world, inside that pampered, carefree body, with smooth arms and hands not roughened by scrubbing with hospital soap. I wanted to be the one seducing Cleo's eyes. "She could have a million freckles under that gown," I blurted out childishly. "The color would filter them out!"

A tiny grin quirked the corner of Cleo's mouth. As always, I wanted to feel the movement of her lips. "Freckles are just fine," she said, "so long as I get to count them." She turned and leaned close, and shivers of anticipation rippled through me. "With my tongue," she added, and very gently laid a trail of tiny wet dots across the bridge of my nose. I forgot entirely where we were.

Then she bent her dark head to my throat, and undid my top buttons, and gently cupped my breasts through my tunic as her warm tongue probed down into the valley between. I couldn't bear to stop her, even when I remembered the guard. My breasts felt heavy, my nipples swollen, but not nearly as heavy and swollen as I needed them to be.

Cleo's gray eyes had darkened when she raised her head. "Where," she murmured huskily, "is a bomb shelter when you need one?"

But we knew that even now, with the Luftwaffe so busy in Hitler's Russian campaign that there hadn't been a really major attack on London in over a year, every bomb shelter had its fiercely protective attendants.

The guard's voice, harsh but muted, startled us. "There's a service lift just down the corridor. It's slow. But not necessarily slow enough."

She gazed impersonally into space, her weathered face expression-less until, as we passed, she glanced down at Cleo's silver wings. "Good work," she said curtly. "I drove an ambulance in France in the last war. But for God's sake, be careful!"

In the elevator Cleo pressed me against a wood-paneled wall and kissed me so hard it hurt. I slid my fingers through her thick dark hair and held her back just enough for my lips to explore the shape of her lips and my tongue to invite hers to come inside.

By the time we jolted to a stop on the ground floor my crotch felt wetter than my mouth, and even more in need of her probing tongue.

There was no one waiting when the gate slid open. Cleo pulled me along until we found a deserted ladies' room, but once inside, she braced her shoulders against the tiled wall and didn't touch me. "You do realize," she said grimly, "what you're risking?"

"Never mind what *I'm* risking," I said. "One nurse blotting her copy book isn't going to bring everything since Florence Nightingale crashing down. But you . . ." I remembered Frank's bitter voice asking, "What kind of woman?" Tears stung my eyes, but it had to be said.

"You're holding history in your hands, Cleo." I reached out to clasp her fingers. "Right where I want to be."

"Are you sure you know what you want?"

"I may not know exactly *what*," I admitted, drawing her hands to my hips, "but I sure as hell know I want it." I reached down and yanked my skirt up as far as I could. Cleo stroked my inner thigh, and I caught my breath; then she slid cool fingers inside my cotton underpants and gently cupped my hot, wet flesh. I moaned and thrust against her touch, and tried to kiss her, but her mouth moved under mine into a wide grin.

"Pretty convincing," she murmured against my lips.

I whimpered as she withdrew her hand, but she just smoothed down my skirt and gave me a pat on my butt. "Not here," she said, and propelled me out the door.

On the long series of bus rides back to Charles Street we tried not to look at each other, but I felt Cleo's dark gaze on me from time to time. I kept my eyes downcast, the better to glance sidelong at her as she alternated between folding her arms across her chest and clenching and unclenching her hands on her blue wool slacks.

Dinner was being served at the Red Cross Club, probably the best meal for the price in England. Cleo muttered that she wasn't hungry, not for dinner, anyway, but I had my own motive for insisting. The band would be setting up in half an hour or so, and with the window open, you could hear the music from my room. Well enough for dancing.

So we ate, although I couldn't say what, and Cleo teased me by running her tongue sensuously around the lip of a Coke bottle and into its narrow throat. Her mercurial shifts from intensity to playfulness fascinated me, but the time came when intensity was all I craved.

"I don't suppose you'd like to dance, would you?" I repeated last night's invitation in a barely steady voice. "If I tried my best to do it right?" I stood abruptly and started for the stairs. Behind me, Cleo's chair fell over with a clatter as she jumped up to follow.

I reached my tiny room ahead of her—nursing builds strong legs. I crossed to the window to heave it open, and then the door slammed shut and she was behind me, pressing her crotch against my ass, wrapping her arms around me to undo my buttons and cradle my breasts through my sensible cotton slip. I longed to be wearing sheer flame-colored silk for her.

When she slid her hands under the fabric and over my skin, though, I found I didn't want to be wearing anything at all. "So soft," she whispered, "so tender . . ." and then, as my nipples jerked taut under her strokes, "and getting so hard . . ."

A melody drifted from below: "Something To Remember You By." I turned in her arms. "Teach me to dance," I whispered.

We swayed gently together, feet scarcely moving in the cramped space, thighs pressing into each other's heat. Cleo kneaded my ass, while I held her so tightly against my breast that her silver wings dented my flesh.

"Please," I murmured against her cheek, "closer . . ." I fumbled at the buttons of her tunic. When she tensed, I drew back. "I'm sorry . . . I don't know the rules . . ."

"The only rule," Cleo said, after a long pause, "is that you get what you need."

"I need to feel you," I said.

She drew her hands over my hips and up my sides until she held my breasts again; then she stepped back and began to shed her clothes. Mine, with a head start, came off even faster.

The heady musk of arousal rose around us. A clarinet crooned, "I'll Get By." I cupped my full breasts and raised them so that my nipples could flick against Cleo's high, tightening peaks, over and over. The sensation was exquisite, tantalizing. I gave a little whimper, needing more, and she bent to take me into her mouth.

I thought I would burst with wanting. My swollen nipples felt as big as her demanding tongue. Then she worked her hand between my legs, and spread the juices from my cunt up over my straining clit, and my whimpers turned to full-throated moans.

Cleo raised her head. Her kiss muted my cries as she reached past me to shut the window. "Hope nobody's home next door," she muttered, and suddenly we were dancing horizontally on the narrow bed. I arched my hips, rubbing against her thigh, until her mouth moved down over throat and breasts and belly, slowly, too slowly; I wanted to savor each moment, but my need was too desperate. I wriggled and thrashed, and her head sank at last between my thighs, just as it had in my dreams. Her mobile lips drove me into a frenzy of pleading, incoherent cries, until, with her tongue thrusting rhythmically into my cunt, my ache exploded into glorious release.

In the first faint light of morning I woke to feel Cleo's fingers tousling my hair. "If I were an artist I'd paint you just like this," she whispered. "You look like a marmalade cat chock-full of cream."

I stretched, and then gasped as her fingers roused last night's ache into full, throbbing resurgence. "Sure enough," she said with a wicked grin, "plenty of cream. Let's see if I can make you yowl again."

This time I found out what her long, strong fingers could do deep inside me, one at first, then two; by the end of the week I could clutch spasmodically around her whole pumping hand.

Sometimes I think I remember every moment of those days; sometimes everything blurs except the feel of Cleo's hands and mouth and body against mine and the way her eyes could shift suddenly from laughing silver to the dark gray of storm clouds.

We did more sightseeing: the Tower of London, Madam Tussaud's Wax Museum, St. Paul's Cathedral scarred by German bombs. We took boat trips up the Thames to Richmond Park, where we dared to kiss in secluded bits of woodland, and downriver where we held hands across the Greenwich Meridian. One night, in anonymous clothes bought at a flea-market barrow, we even managed to get into a club Cleo had heard of where women did dance openly with women. We couldn't risk staying long, but a dark intoxication followed us back to her room, where I entirely suppressed the nurse in me and demanded things of Cleo that left both of us sore, drained and without regrets.

On our last night in London we went anonymously again into shabby back streets near the docks. I brought disinfectant, and we chose what seemed the cleanest of a sorry lot of tattoo parlors. There, welcoming the pain of the needle as distraction from deeper pain, we had tiny pairs of wings etched over our left breasts.

We parted with promises to meet one more time before Cleo's last flight. I mortgaged a week of sleep to get my nursing shifts covered, and at Hamble Airfield, by moonlight, she introduced me to the planes she loved.

"This is the last Spitfire I'll ever fly," she said, stroking the sleek fuselage. "Seafire III, Merlin 55 engine, twenty-four-thousand-foot ceiling, although I won't go up that far just on a hop to Scotland."

From Scotland she'd catch an empty cargo plane back to the States. I had just got my orders to report to Hawaii for assignment somewhere in the South Pacific. War is hell, and so are goodbyes.

"Could I look into the cockpit?" I asked, wanting to be able to envision her there, high in the sky.

"Sure. You can even sit in it and play pilot, if you like." She helped me climb onto the wing, with more pressing of my ass than was absolutely necessary, and showed me how to lower myself into the narrow space. Standing on the wing, she leaned in and kissed me, hard at first, then with aching tenderness, then hard again.

"Pull up your skirt," she ordered, and I did it without question. She already knew I wasn't wearing underpants. "Let's see how wet you can get the seat, so I can breathe you all the way to Scotland." She unbuttoned my shirt and played with my breasts until I begged her to lean in far enough to suck my aching nipples; then, with her lips and tongue and teeth driving me so crazy that my breath came in a storm of desperate gasps, she reached down into my slippery heat and made me arch and buck so hard that the plane's dials and levers were in danger. I needed more than I could get sitting in the cramped cockpit.

We clung together finally in the grass under the sheltering wing. I got my hands into Cleo's trousers and made her groan, but she wouldn't relax into sobbing release until she had her whole hand at last inside me and I was riding it on pounding waves of pleasure as keen as pain.

I thought, when I could think anything again, that she had fallen asleep, she was so still. Gently, gently, I touched my lips to the nearly healed tattoo above her breast. Tiny wings matching mine. Something to remember her by.

Without opening her eyes she said, in a lost, small voice, "What are we going to do, Kay?"

I knew what she was going to do. "You're going to claim the sky, to make history. And anyway," I said, falling back on dark humor since I had no comfort to offer, "a cozy ménage in Paris seems out of the question with the Nazis in control."

Then, because I knew if I touched her again we would both cry, and hate ourselves for it, I stood, put my clothes in as much order as I could, and walked away.

I looked back once, from the edge of the field. Cleo leaned, head bowed, against the plane. Some trick of the moonlight transmuted her dark hair into silver; I had a vision of how breathtaking she would be in thirty or forty years. The pain of knowing I couldn't share those years made me stumble, and nearly fall. But I kept on walking.

And she let me go.

In June of 1944, against all justice and reason, the bill to make the Women's Airforce Service Pilots officially part of the Army Air Forces was defeated in Congress by nineteen votes. In December, the WASPs were disbanded. By then, though, after going through hell in the Pacific Theater, I had met Jack, who truly loved and needed me, whose son was growing below my heart. His kisses tasted of home, and peace, and more unborn children demanding their chance at life.

Thirty-three years later, in 1977, when women were at last being admitted into the Air Force, the WASPs were retroactively given military status. It was then, through a reunion group, that I found out what had become of Cleo Remington; she had found a sky high and wide enough to hold her fierce spirit, and freedom as a bush pilot in Alaska.

And she was, as I discovered, even more breathtaking at sixty than she'd been at twenty-six.

But that's another chapter of the story.

Jaclyn Friedman

DEEPER

We had been lovers just long enough to memorize each other's scent. He wore his under his cologne; you had to get close to his skin to smell it. Grass. New-cut pine. Fox fur. It didn't matter now. My roommate was inside, waiting for him to go so she and I could begin eviscerating him while we ate the leftover mushroom quiche.

Except there was his hand. The pads of his thin, long fingers pressing through the metal mesh of the screen door. Still touching me, only now in tiny diamond shapes, so many bits of him straining mutely toward me. Heat. I touched my fingertips to his, pressed our palms together. No matter how hard I pressed, he would eventually go. God, I wanted him. Not just physically. I wanted him to make me whole.

We weren't meant to be lovers. He was a freshman, nineteen and pimply. President of the Young Republicans, to boot. We weren't even what you would call friends, just amicable campus politicos. We would catch a slice of pizza together on occasion after meetings to rehash and strategize. He would update me on his deteriorating relationship with his sweet blonde girlfriend, and I would dispense big-sisterly advice.

This is how all the stories start. "We weren't meant to be lovers. Then one day . . . "

One day a guy I barely knew climbed into my bed and got on top of me. One day he wouldn't stop even when I said no. It doesn't take long for the landscape to change. It doesn't take long for something small inside you to break, like the filament of a light bulb.

And then one day a few months later there was Scott, standing next to me on the bricked-in terrace on top of the campus center. We were watching the stars emerge, admiring the glow of Venus, or maybe it was Jupiter. The sweet swollen smell of spring in New England was in our noses. There was the size of him, not bulky but tall, solid, safe, his hands large and gentle. He was saying he wished he could take my pain away; this, after I spilled my guts to him, after he noticed I was not okay, after he asked, after I told him what I could of the truth. He said, "If I could, I would carry your pain," and I gave it to him that night, not even deciding to, not even knowing that I had, just sliding it off my heart and giving it to him, the way you shed wet clothes after the rain, glad to be light and naked and to have the chance to dry in the air. The way you laugh as you peel them off, skin tickling, and you run to lie under the fans and kiss and get wet all over again.

Like that. And kissing him was the least and the greatest of the pleasures that followed, and we did it often after that first night. And there were his hands on my breasts in that new way, the way hands touch your breasts when they are not used to it, when they are just learning the particular dimensions of your curves and the way your breath catches when they stroke the dark areola just next to the nipple, when they are learning how hard and large your nipples get with the slightest encouragement, and how your body sighs into those hands when they take up the weight of your breast, cupping the underneath of them.

Do you remember sleeping with someone in a single bed? It's not like we wanted to sleep much, but it was nearly finals and we were both pretty conscientious students. Maybe we slept three hours that first night, me tucked between his body and the wall. It had taken us a solid hour to work up the nerve to kiss, even though we both knew that's what I'd come for, scurrying across campus to find him after I missed him at the late movie. He had waited for me at the early one.

The kiss was warm and awkward and electric, the way first kisses can be. His lips were thick and I felt enveloped by them, stroked and held. He traced his hands up the curves of my arms to my shoulders, then pressed them gently into the center of my back. His mouth slid down the left side of my neck, and the wet pressure of his tongue sent a single shiver through me. My body bent toward him, almost imperceptibly. He returned his mouth to mine, bringing his hands with him, running his fingertips across my face and sinking them deep in my tangle of hair. Something else broke inside me then, a chain on a gate, and hunger was free, and we kissed on that narrow bed until nothing existed but lips on skin.

I broke my own rules with him, begged him to enter me on only the fourth night we were together. I was tired of feigning control. I couldn't pretend I was sane anymore, or that every entryway into me was not already open to him. When he came to bed I was already naked, swollen. It took very little time for him to undress. He kissed me slowly, took time to greet my belly, my breasts, my neck, the curve of my ass. He broke the seal of my cunt lips with his index finger, sliding through the wet heat of me, fingering my hole. I reached for the condom I had set out beside the lamp on my night table and unwrapped it. He took it from me and I watched as he slid it on. His cock was long and smooth, about as thick as my wrist. I had already cradled it in my mouth, sucked it, felt it throb hot against my tongue as I slid my lips down the length of it and back. I had already seen his face as I did this, watched it soften and harden with the rhythm of my strokes, braced as he shot into me, his hands buried in my hair, holding my head where he needed it most. I needed him now, needed him to burn me clean of everything that had happened. I needed him to make me precious again.

And he obliged. He slid into me and I have never felt so perfect as when my hips tilted up to greet him. *Yes, take me, make me yours, yes, please god, make it never have happened, make everything be about this moment, make me forget everything but your cock in me, pushing through my deepest folds, your heat and my heat burning into each other until we scar.* He fucked me slowly, almost thoughtfully, each stroke plunging deeper, pushing harder, than the last. My clit throbbed.

As his cock slid home (*home!*) again and again he kissed me everywhere; my lips of course, his tongue strong and hungry in my mouth; my neck, tenderly behind my ears; my shoulder; the inside of my elbow. Then, abruptly, he stopped, and I could see that his cock was all he could feel, sliding, sliding, the dripping walls of my pussy stroking every millimeter of him, faster, faster, and it was all I could feel, too, the way the pleasure took him over, the way he needed my body more than breath in that moment, the way my pussy was once again a holy land.

I made him picnics of cheese and bread and cheap wine, and we ate them beneath the enormous willow tree behind the science center. He confessed his love of Elton John, and we spent nights in the heat of the attic apartment he'd rented for the summer, listening to *Goodbye Yellow Brick Road* and *Madman across the Water* with the lights out. We snuck onto the nearby Putt-Putt course and played at midnight, crawling around under windmills and giant plastic squirrels in order to find the balls in the dark, making it to the fifteenth tee before succumbing to our preference to put better things in holes than little bits of pock-marked green and blue plastic. We did it everywhere we could get our hands on each other: on the kitchen counter and in the kitchen sink, against chalkboards at the apexes of abandoned lecture halls, sloshing around in the depths of the clawfoot tub in the professor's house I was looking after. Deeper and deeper and deeper.

And then, the note. It was in the kind of envelope meant to mail checks in, and I knew everything as soon as I saw it, before I even turned it over to read my name in his telltale scrawl.

In hindsight, I don't think he had ever stopped thinking of her. While they had been struggling ever since he started school the previous fall, they had split up for good only a few weeks before our lips first touched. When he mentioned one night that he'd been speaking to her again I told him it was cool, I understood. He had the right to talk with whomever he liked.

That night he took me on my knees from behind, and I was grateful to be reduced to my most animal form. His body eclipsed mine as he reached for my clit, stroking me with the flat of his finger and riding me hard, his cock thrusting over and over again against the walls of my cunt as I closed around him, his balls slapping against my thighs. His entire weight pressed into me each time he sank in, and I felt contained by it, held in. My clit swelled for him and he took it between his fingers and rolled it, stroking the entire circumference, pressing just hard enough to make the moan that was gathering in my belly escape low and long through my throat. He was grunting now, each time his shaft drove into me, *uh, uh,* an escalating punctuation. My pussy opened toward him with each stroke of his cock inside me, each stroke of his finger on my clit. We were going to come, both of us were moving there, I could feel us rising together, spurring each other toward climax. He shot first, his hips sinking into my ass as his cock heaved deeper still into the depths of me and stayed there, shuddering and pulsing. He grabbed my clit harder as he came and I broke against him, the convulsions of my cunt clamping down around his cock, releasing, seizing him again, milking him into me, locking our passions together until we collapsed sweaty on the bed and slept there, curled into each other like bear cubs.

And then.

Six days later there was only the porch screen between us. We had already said our goodbyes. He had apologized. We had both expressed regrets. He wished there were two of him, so he didn't have to choose. I wished I had met him sooner, before she had taken root in his heart. I didn't hate him. Not yet.

We stood like that a long time, our hands pressed together like a prayer. It could have been an hour. I don't remember if we spoke. I can't imagine what I would have said. I didn't know what was to come. I couldn't have described to him what it feels like for pain to slide back into your heart like a dark storm that rains tears and thunder through you for days. I couldn't have told him how, after he left, I would make it just inside the front door before sliding to the floor of the stairwell, sobbing so deeply I could not hear myself, so hard it brought my roommate running with phone in hand, abandoning the quiche to the humidity and the cats. I could not have explained how the world would go gray for months, how autumn that year would not touch me, even with its magic periwinkle dusks, how it would be spring again before I would remember that there was even a door inside me I could open.

I wish I could have told him what a gift it was to have had someone carry the weight of my grief, even for a while. I wish either of us could have known the price I would pay for that luxury. Instead, I told him it was later than either of us had noticed, and that maybe he should go. He stayed there for a minute longer, barely breathing, and then he brought his face to the screen and we let our lips touch through the tiny openings. And then I felt his face pull away, and the night air on my hands, and he turned to face the street.

Lucy Moore

I CAN STILL SMELL YOU

When I open the box, the scent rushes up at me, thick and full. I close my eyes, let the smells trickle through my hair and my eyelashes, swirl around me like mist. This box, the box holding the memories of you and me, a time capsule of dead love, has been closed for years. So why can I still smell you as though you were standing behind me?

As I push back the flaps, the cardboard scrapes against my palms. A warning, perhaps. I lift a packet of letters, wrapped in faded pink ribbon, and press them to my lips, breathing deeply. The smell of your cologne burns my skin. Under the letters, a denim shirt, faded soft with washing, shrunk too small for you, but so big on me it hung over my hands when I made you breakfast on Saturdays. I kiss that too, and smell detergent, the veil of fabric softener and you.

I put down the letters and slip the shirt over my head, letting the sleeves slide down my arms. The fabric raises the soft hairs there. I pull the front together, button it loosely around me. As I shift back toward the box, the fabric grazes my breasts and I shudder. Burying my face in the shirt, I let a few tears slide down my face, sink themselves in the weave of the fabric, and then I can smell salt, and I can taste you again.

The last time I wore this shirt, it was still good. When I woke up, you were sleeping beside me, a flash of blonde hair spread out on the pillow, your lips open wide. Your breath whistled out hot and slightly sour. I watched you sleep, listened to you snore until I couldn't hold back my giggles and slid gently out of bed, careful not to wake you. The shirt was lying on the back of the chair in our bedroom, and I put it on, yanking a pair of panties from the laundry basket. The clothes had been clean for days, but you never got around to putting them away.

As I tiptoed toward the door, skipping the board that always squeaked, my thighs twinged pleasantly. I could smell the traces of your cologne on my skin, the sticky sharpness between my thighs, the wet heat of your tongue on my ears. I smiled again as I closed the bedroom door, letting you sleep, and another rush of our pleasantly mingled sweat teased my nose.

Passover had come and gone, so the bakery had made challah that Friday. I could never resist that thick, buttery smell, and the way the braided loaves glistened in the bakery window. The storefront always looked so forlorn during that empty week of unleavened bread, and when the first loaves appeared after the holiday, I wanted to roll among them, feeling the soft crust peel off and press against my skin, the thick, doughy scent tattooing my nose. But usually I just settled for two loaves, wrapped in a white paper sack that went waxy where the butter stained it.

Saturday mornings meant French toast. In the kitchen, I turned on NPR and let the sound drift by as I filled the air with the noise of cooking. Eggs beaten pale daffodil, creamy whole milk, the plastic jug of maple syrup warming on the stove. Fresh oranges crushed into juice, the pulp strained out just the way you liked it, and peaches sliced into bowls, the pits, frayed with flesh, in the trash.

I always saved slicing the bread for last. Back then, no one had heard of low-carb diets. I long for those days sometimes, when I walk by a Jewish bakery. The slicing was a pleasant ritual, hesitantly pressing the knife against the end, the crust breaking and fluttering as I sawed gently. Challah will flatten, the air pushed out, if you press too hard while you cut, so I had perfected the way I did it, slicing off the heels and then cutting straight into the center.

That morning I paused, as I always did, just after cutting the middle of the loaf, and let the smell wash over me, slightly sweet, slightly yeasty, yellow-dark. I ran my fingertips over the slick crust, reading the bumps of the braids like Braille, and smiled. "I missed you," I whispered.

"Mmm, I missed you too," you whispered, slipping your hands under my shirttails and covering my stomach as you kissed my neck.

I laughed, turning my head so I could kiss your mouth, tasting the slight tint of peppermint. "I was talking to the bread," I said, and then laughed when you cocked an eyebrow at me. "You shouldn't have brushed your teeth. I made orange juice."

You took a swallow and grimaced at the combination. "It'll wear off." I nodded, and slipped the knife back into the bread as you picked up the paper, rubbing your hands through your hair as you scanned the front page. When you sat down, I watched you for a moment, my hands sorting the slices of bread with the knowledge of a lover. The morning sun burned through the pale curtains and your hair shone bright as a star. Your chest was bare, the gentle curls of hair tracing over and down into the sweatpants you'd tied loosely around your hips, the jut of your hipbones persuading me.

I remember what you were wearing, what you looked like that morning, because I was thinking, at that moment, that you had never looked more handsome, and I had never loved you more.

When you looked up, you caught me standing and watching, and you winked. "I'm hungry," you said.

"Oops, sorry." I busied myself dipping the soft bread into the egg mixture, letting it sit for a moment, filling the tiny hollows with thick liquid, and then putting each slice into the pan to sizzle. But when I flipped the first batch onto a plate and carried it to you at the table, you caught me before I could walk away.

Lifting my shirt, you pressed a kiss just below my belly button, catching my hips in your hands. The wet pressure of your tongue dipped down under the elastic of my plain cotton panties, and I felt a matching moisture purr its way between my thighs. "I can still smell myself on you," you said thickly, your hands pushing my panties down.

On the stove, the pan was spitting angrily, but I simply stepped out of my panties and kicked them aside as you spread my legs with your wide, slender hands, and buried your nose between my thighs. You inhaled, and I laughed, as I always did. I have never met a man who loved the scent of me the way you did, and never one who reveled so much in the combination of our smells. I had always hated the stale smell of sex until I met you and you woke me with your face buried between my thighs, just breathing.

"You're wet," you whispered, and your breath pushed me apart, my knees getting a little weak. Before I could answer, you stuck your tongue out, dragging it along the split of my vulva, soft pink kissing soft pink, sucking out yesterday. I pushed down on your shoulders, arching forward as I felt the heat of your skin rise.

The smell was incredible. The bread, the peaches, and then you and me. I moved one of my hands onto your chest, teasing the flat nipple until it stood up, pressing back insistently against my nails, and then I tugged sharply. You gasped, pushing your tongue inside me, and then you started to flick harder, sucking my clit into your mouth and dragging your teeth along the underside.

I was on the edge when you pulled back, but I wasn't disappointed. How many times had we made love by then? Hundreds? Thousands? We had rhythms, you and I, rhythms for grocery shopping, for paying the bills, for making love. You knew I wouldn't come like that. I sat down on your lap, straddling you, and we kissed. I could taste the acrid remnants of last night and the softer flavor of this morning. My thighs protested as I moved forward, but I ignored them, focusing on the way your hands tugged the buttons of my shirt apart, and then you pulled your mouth from mine and kissed me lower.

As your lips and teeth and tongue worked a pattern over my breasts, tugging at my thick nipples, leaving a slug's trail over the smooth undersides, I moved my hands down, finding the bulge under the soft cotton of your sweatpants. You were so hard, and we had only made love a few hours ago. I had to pull at the loose fabric until I found the cords that tightened the pants around your waist, and then I was touching you, feeling a hot, hard bar against my palms.

When I ran my thumb over the head, I could hear you whisper my name against my breasts, sounding so soft and vulnerable. Your hand worked between my thighs, two fingers on my clit, moving in a slow circle, and I curled my toes, trying to remember not to grip your cock too hard. I let myself breathe, inhaling my own scent, stronger than the smells of cooking. You worked your lips over my nipples, sucking, flicking your tongue back and forth, and then imitating the motion of your fingers on my clit. I was jerking you off, not even knowing it, concentrating, thinking about all the things that made me come: your breath hot in my ear while you told me how you wanted to fuck me, your finger in my ass as you ate me out, your cock in my mouth as you pumped your hips back and forth.

"Oh god, oh god, oh god, oh fuck," I said, not even hearing myself. I tore my hand away from your cock, grabbed your wrist and held your fingers still. Your mouth stilled and your fingers stopped, pressed hard against me, letting me come in a firm pulse against your hand. A trickle of stale semen slipped out of my pussy, relict of our earlier union, oozing down into the cleft between my ass cheeks, and I started to laugh.

"Good?" you asked, with a little-boy grin as you pulled your mouth from my breast and smiled up at me.

"Yes, good," I answered, and kissed you on the mouth, softly, tenderly, tasting myself again. I still had one hand on your cock, but I didn't feel sexy anymore, I felt like going for a run. Or like falling asleep. But I owed you one. "Would you like to eat your breakfast?" I asked. "Or would you like me to take care of this?" I gave your cock a squeeze, ran my thumb over the head and pushed the moisture around until it dried.

You kissed me again. "I'm going to eat while you save that pan from burning."

I looked up, and sure enough the acrid smell of burning butter was rising from the pan on the stove. "Shit," I said, jumping off your lap and running for the stove. I flipped the too-long sleeve of my shirt down over my hand and moved the pan to another burner. You laughed, coming over to the stove to grab the syrup from the pan of warm water, and kissed my neck before heading back to the table.

We ate together, me feeling dreamy and happy from my orgasm, and I watched you. It was one of those moments I wanted to hold on to, wanted to think of when I held our future children. You lifted your hand to rub your temple, and left a smear of newsprint on your forehead. I laughed out loud, so stupidly happy, and you caught my hand, kissed my palm. "I love you," you said.

"Then fuck me," I said, laughing again. I pushed your plate back, the newspaper fluttering to the floor, and pulled my shirt open again as I climbed onto the table, sitting in front of you. You kicked your chair back and pulled your cock out, and I stroked it hard as we kissed again, feeling the pumping rise of your flesh under my fingers. I felt like a porn star, like the sexiest woman alive, as your cock grew under my touch and your hands grasped my hips, pulling me forward on the table.

The nudge of your cock head between my cunt lips made me sigh with pleasure, and my thighs protested again as I spread them wide, hooking my feet together behind you, pulling you in hard. I wouldn't come this time, but it didn't matter. I just wanted to have you fuck me on our kitchen table, feel the length of you pushing against me, inside me, as you grunted with pleasure. The smell of challah and syrup was thick in your hair as you lowered your head to my shoulder as you pushed deeper, your nails branding my skin. I moaned with pleasure, listened to the catch in your breath when I did. I could taste peaches and my own wetness, and when you pushed three long, slow thrusts into me, I could feel your cock pumping in orgasm.

When you pulled out, I tried to kiss you again, but you were looking for my panties, handing them to me before the soft white trickle from inside me covered the table. I stepped into the cotton again, and kissed your neck before I picked up my bowl of peaches and took them over to the sink, where I ate them as I did the dishes, as you sat at the table finishing the paper. My lips were coated with juice, my thighs were sticky with come, and when I got in the shower, I found your newsprint handprint on my thigh.

It has been three years since I saw you, three years since I heard you say my name, three years since us. I sometimes wonder what I would say if I saw you again—if I would say all the things I've written in my journal all these years, or if I would just say hello.

I realize I am still crying, and I blow my nose on the corner of the shirt and wipe my eyes with the sleeve. I hold my nose there, in the crook of my elbow, breathing slowly as the tears come slower. It's all there in the fabric—the syrup, the challah and you. And I know what I would say if I saw you again.

Number One

I had no idea what I was doing, no real idea what was supposed to be happening. Either I managed to fake enough nonchalance or she was just polite enough not to mention it. I'd never been with a woman before. She used to be in the Army. For months I watched the slight rise of her bound breasts, wishing she'd let me touch them or even see them.

She was almost old enough to be my mother and she taught me how to kiss. I had kissed boys before. But not like this. And I remember thinking: *Whoa. No stubble.*

We fucked as often as I'd let her slide a hand under my skirt, except for the day I wore jeans and she scowled until she took me home. I didn't know I was supposed to be the femme. All I knew was she was experienced and I wanted to do to her the things she did to me. But she was very good at distraction. I spent a lot of time on my back.

Finally one day she let me, on a hot August afternoon, and the sweat on the buzzed-short back of her neck tasted good under my mouth when she finally let me get her on her hands and knees and fuck her from behind. She bucked hard against my hand, trying to get me to give her more, and more, as I bit my way down her back through her shivers and sweat, my hand mysteriously sliding almost all the way inside her. "Harder, harder," she grunted, cunt so tense around my fingers I thought she'd snap them off. She came once, hard and fast, and never mentioned it again.

Number Two

Fumbling, we fell onto the lumpy dorm room bed. She didn't know what to do any better than I did, but she was blonde and Southern and slightly drunk and she wore lip-gloss that stained my pillowcase. I could've lived between her breasts, full and fair and jiggly in a way that made them look like they were balanced on the noses of two trained seals. We kissed for hours as the alcohol wore off, and then she surprised me by asking me, sober but squirming, to help her take her jeans off.

She tasted like the first sip of a margarita and she had a drawl when she whimpered "oh jayzus don't stop" and I barely got two fingers into her before she yowled like a cat and came so hard she almost broke my nose with her pubic bone.

The next night, I learned when to get my head the hell out of the way.

Number Three

"Nah, it's okay," I said, knowing it had to be even if it wasn't really. She looked half relieved, half still worried as she reached out to touch my hand. "I knew you guys were probably going to get back together. You've done this sort of thing before. You have a blowup, then get back together. It's okay."

She leaned forward and kissed me on the cheek, daring a smile.

"Just one thing, though," I added, feeling the need to remind her that she'd wanted me, that his dick didn't make him better, just easier. She arched an eyebrow. "What's that?"

"I give better head than he does."

"Yes, you do." She shifted her weight. I met her gaze and didn't say a word, waiting until the silence filled the air between our bodies.

"Don't . . . " she began, and then stopped. Her fingers were small and desperate as she took my hand and lifted it, pressed it against her mound through the itchy tweed of her skirt. "Give me something to remember you by?"

Like she always did, she bucked and whimpered, pouted, gasped, purred. And like she always did she hit the point where she begged me to hurt her, to bite her, to use her, to rip her open, to make her come.

I never found out what her fiancé had to say about the welts from my teeth, curved and purple, that spotted her thighs, her ass, the shaven smoothness of her pussy. But fuck it. I only gave her what she asked for.

Number Four

It took me ages to realize she wanted to kiss me. I just thought she had a weird way of standing, sort of angling herself toward me, looking up at me with big wide hopeful eyes. I was actually much more interested in her husband, but she was cute and smart and in the ashes of so much desolation I guessed she'd do.

And she did, for a while. I worked myself numb on her, so small in my arms that I could lift her ass up with two hands, feeding her into my mouth like a tart as I coaxed my thumb between her tiny ass cheeks. I fucked her hard, past the point where she cried that she couldn't come again. "No, no more," she'd squeal, trying to wriggle out of reach, forgetting that I was twice her size, that I could lift her, pin her, hold her precisely where I wanted her even with only one arm. "No, no, please," she'd sob as she spread her legs wider, as she gripped my hands and forced my fingers to dig even deeper into her doll-sized hips as I held her firm against my mouth, sucking her, licking her. "No, no, no," she would cry, the cries rising higher and higher, keening, and I would shove three fingers into her just at the end to make her scream, hoping that maybe this time her cries would drown out the din in my heart. I wore myself out on her, on her hunger, on her false resistance, but my arms never ached enough to blot out the way it felt to hold the one before.

"No, no," she cried on our last afternoon together, and she wept real tears. Then I closed the door on her and on my shame, and took my grief elsewhere.

Number Five

"Goddamn it," she said, "will you shut up about it already?"

I knew her tone, and I knew what it meant, and I closed my mouth in midsentence as her hands found the zipper on the back of my skirt and peeled it open over the crack of my ass. A trail of moist kiss-prints down my spine cooled me down, anger dissolving into the wet of her tongue as she probed the crease at the top of my ass. Fingers found my cunt, another hand pushed me over the arm of the couch, face first into the cushions. She worked a cock into me, fucking me slow as clover honey as she lubed my ass and slapped a dam between my spread cheeks. Her tongue snaked into my ass on a slick of angel grease, and I shuddered so hard I thought my spine would snap at the filthy glory of every forbidden reentry.

"Fuck me, please fuck me," I begged, and she refused so she could hear me beg again, so she could stop my breath midword with a sudden stab of her agile tongue, a sharp twist of the silicone cock deep against my cervix. Hours later she wore me tight around her wrist like a gauntlet, the only noise from my ruined throat a rasp like silk-stockinged thighs against one another, a desperate "Yes, yes" to everything, to the fist in my cunt, to the fourth finger that stretched my ass, to the look in her eyes that taught me to be grateful to be broken.

Number Six

I saw it coming long before she did. At the club that night I knew it was near, saw the thunderhead in the air, shimmering fury like the air above an August highway, and then she stormed away and back to the chair next to mine, slamming down into the seat and making her martini slosh onto the table.

"Well, that's that," she said, sighing and gulping, then plucking the olive off the plastic sword with pale, sharp-looking teeth.

"Single again?"

She nodded.

"Makes two of us," I said, carefully directing my words to the lime twist on the rim of my glass. "First time you and I have ever been single at the same time, I think."

She looked at me to see if I meant what my tone implied. I grinned over the rim of my cosmopolitan, took the flower out of the vase on the table, tucked it behind her ear into the mist-white of her hair. I admired the albino delicacy of her skin, the map of her veins below the surface of the curves that disappeared into her dress. She licked her lips at me. I licked her lips back, savoring the mixture of lipstick and gin.

"Shall we?" she asked, handing me my bag. And we did, her lipstick smearing a comet tail up the inside of my thigh, long enough and loud enough that the neighbors eventually gave up banging on the wall with a broom handle.

Number Seven

She was good, very good, good enough to leave me gasping just with the merest hint that she might pull my head back that way, her fingers knotted in the hair at the nape of my neck. She knew how to bite me and make me writhe, and she knew how to work herself into me so that all I could say when she tucked her thumb inside was "please." She wore me like a mink, took me cruising on her bike, put a collar around my neck and made me lick my wetness from the saddle at the rest area while she took pictures, my bare ass under that too-short skirt feeling the breeze when I bent over to lick my cream from the leather. She was tall and dark and had dreads down to her ass and my god, she had the longest fingers I have ever seen.

"Some days," she said to me once, "I feel like there's not a femme in the world I can't get right down on her knees, begging me to give it to her just one more time."

And you know, she was *almost* right.

Would it be sexist to say that June Cleaver or Donna Reed wouldn't be so bad to have waiting for me when I got home? Or maybe a nice little Jeannie?"

"Only if you've got a dick, and I don't think you're packing at the moment," my boyfriend replied.

"I'm not. So I'll say it: I could learn to live with having a chilled martini, a home-cooked meal, a cute little apron and heels waiting for me."

Finn slipped his feet up on the coffee table and pulled a long draw from his ale. "Huh. So, you're saying that all this old-fashioned egalitarian stuff just isn't doing it for you?"

"Oh no. Most of the time it does, and besides, I don't really know how you do it the other way when there are lofts and starving artists and tofu and multiculturalism and secondary partners involved. Hell, we don't even have a tablecloth."

"Not really necessary when you don't have a table to put it on."

"Now, you know, that's the truth," I acknowledged, propping my feet up next to Finn's and digging into my takeout Thai food.

He took another long swig, then dug the rest of the pad Thai out from the bottom of the cardboard container, munching as he spoke.

"Maybe Joe'd do it."

I barely managed to keep peanut sauce from shooting out of my nose as I snorted with laughter. "Oh yeah, she'd go for that. We'll just have to tell her to leave her hacksaw at the door."

I will reluctantly confess that at the time of the events I am relating, my life was something of a late-twentieth-century cliché. I had a boyfriend who stayed home and manned the fort (as it were), making postmodern art, and a girlfriend named Joe who was a carpenter. We barely managed a totally disorganized pansexual, interracial, age-disparate polyamorous relationship. I ran a dingy coffeeshop in the greedy, looming shadow of Starbucks, which means I catered mainly to the Finns and Joes of the world, as well as the young folks who think they want to be the Finns and Joes of the world, only with the benefit of a trust fund to back them up. We lived in a loft with a bathtub in the kitchen, in a neighborhood that inevitably became gentrified by the time we got ready to move out. We were all vegan and we often put the wrong person's Doc Martens in the morning. Our cat, a stray that moved in without checking the lease or seeing the vet first, was named Sisyphus. I swear to god, none of this was particularly intentional. It just sorta happened.

"You have a point," Finn replied, acknowledging the difficulties inherent in dealing with a lover who occasionally insisted on a quickie whilst still attired in a toolbelt.

"Now, you, on the other hand," I mused, "are another story. With those hips, you know, you'd look dashing in an apron."

Finn stood up and looked himself over. "Gosh, you think? You don't think my ass is too flat?"

"Nah, a few homemade potato-chip casseroles and you'll put Gina Lollobrigida to shame."

He vamped it up, puckering his lips at me. "Well, aren't you a peach."

I eyed the kitchen as he tossed his takeout container in the trash with far less than NBA-caliber aim, knocking a shower of slimy bean sprouts from the black trash bag to the mangy floor. The dishes leered at me from their overgrown pile. I flipped the TV set off with the remote.

Finn flopped into the bathtub, slopping water on the floor. Again. The cat leapt onto my lap, gouging my thighs in the process, I felt my eyeballs roll far back enough into my head to see the times tables I memorized in the third grade.

Ayiyi! Where was June Cleaver when a girl needed her, I ask you?

"Can I get a half-caf carob enriched soy mocha, no whip, with froth?"

I gestured to the espresso machine behind the counter, turning a page. "Be my guest."

He just stood there. Oy, the lost of the world that ended up on my doorstep. I gave him a glare over my dog-eared copy of Marcuse.

"*Neshomeleh*, this is not a service clinic for the obsessive-compulsive, I don't have an insurance plan or scheduled breaks, nor does coffee itself do squat for me at this point. You want a coffee, I can get you a coffee. You want a Martha Stewart special that's basically just coffee with a bunch of weird shit thrown in *exactly* the way you like it, you're more than welcome to make it yourself, but I refuse to be an enabler."

A beat or two skipped. "You know, a strong cup of coffee with a lot of cream would be perfect."

Bella's Cafe and Consumer Rehabilitation Clinic. Over five customers cured daily. "That's my guy. I'm on it."

As I switched the old basket of grounds for a new one, I noticed out of the corner of my eye that Finn was attempting to snatch one of my tables and get it out the door. I ran around the counter and blocked the entrance, a flash of hoop earrings and vintage 1970s polyester, hopefully managing to look forbidding as well as fashionable. "No way, Finn. Not again."

He dropped the table and put his hands up. "Caught red-handed by Foxy Brownstein, the caffeine police! I surrender! Unless you have a billy club, in which case I could put up a little struggle for fun . . ."

I wasn't falling for it. "You know what I'm talking about, Finn. I'm not losing another table so that you can glue it to the ceiling again. Not only did the last one not sell, but I lost a table and nearly half my foot when it got humid. No."

He shifted on his feet. "What if I promise to obey the laws of gravity and good taste?"

I looked at him sidelong, waving a hand in approval at my newly cured patient who was reaching to refill his own cup. "It's the gravity part that concerns me. Will we see this table again tomorrow, legs and all?"

"Scout's honor." Finn performed a rather involved hand gesture, then picked up the table and walked out.

The patient slurped his java and gave me a sympathetic look. "I don't think that was the Scout hand signal."

I doubted it myself. "Maybe in Sicily."

I dragged my sorry ass up three flights of stairs to find Joe leaning against the wall drumming "Wipe Out" on her knees. You know, maybe I don't get to come home to Donna Reed, but coming home to find your sweaty, dreadlocked girlfriend waiting for you in a dirty tank top and jack boots isn't so bad, either. I fought off the urge to start singing "Hey Joe," and just wolf whistled instead.

Joe smiled and planted a salty kiss on my lips. "You know, your boyfriend's a total freak. He paged me and told me to come in time for dinner tonight, and now he won't let me in."

I put my hands to my mouth, trying to look surprised. "Oy gevalt! And he always seemed so normal! How do I always end up with these guys?"

Joe shrugged, grinning, and grabbed my ass. As I jumped, I heard the stereo start rolling out Herb Alpert. Joe and I each raised an eyebrow. In unison. Then the door opened.

"Holy shit," we said, also in unison. We were getting good at this. Joe dropped her viselike grip on my left buttock.

Finn stood in the doorway, a hand on his hip . . . which supported his apron. Which covered a gorgeous black silk cocktail dress. Which stopped at Cuban-heeled stockings that disappeared into classic black patent-leather pumps. He winked at me from beneath a false eyelash.

Joe put a hand on my shoulder, her mouth hanging open. "Well good golly, Miss Molly."

Finn swiveled on his heel, gesturing into the loft. "Don't stand outside all night, I know you've both had a very long day. Why don't you give me your coats and have a seat?"

It was August and we didn't have coats, but no matter. Joe and I moved slowly inside. Joe elbowed me in the ribs. "You forget to medicate him this morning?"

I shook my head. "No. But I think I'm responsible anyway. I'll explain later."

We slid onto the sofa while I tried to figure out if that was really a vacuum cleaner I saw in the corner, and if so, from which of our friends Finn possibly could have borrowed such a contraption. Joe scratched her head, watching as Finn did something or other in the kitchen.

"You know, I have to say this," Joe murmured. "Finn looks . . . well, Finn looks completely fuckable."

And now I have to press Pause again. Joe and Finn got along just fine, and we'd dabbled a few times in some synchronized shtupping, but Joe was around mainly because she was attracted to me. Finn happened to have some extra equipment that she occasionally found useful. But "occasionally useful" and "fuckable" are not one and the same.

I think I blinked at her. But before I could get too confused, my newly femme boyfriend came and whisked us both off the couch. "We'll be having our drinks on the patio this evening."

I was starting to earnestly worry about him. "That's nice, bubbe," I said as soothingly as possible. "Except . . . we don't have a patio."

He clucked his tongue at me and rubbed my shoulder a bit, steering me toward the back of the loft. "Poor Bella. She must have had a really hard day. We do have a patio, darling," he said, turning me toward a crudely built platform upon which sat my table, fully set, and behind which was a full wall mural of a suburban backyard. Of course, you'd only have known that's what it was if you'd been familiar with Finn's particular artistic style. Otherwise, you might have thought it was a spotty green wall that got hit with an overturned dumpster. But I have a knack for artistic interpretation.

He held out a chair for each of us as we slid into them, both of us unusually silent. Truth is, I was fixated on Finn's ass swathed in black silk. And I wasn't the only one. I was also fixated on Joe, who was likewise fixated on Finn's ass swathed in black silk. He looked way better than June Cleaver ever did.

"Martini, Ward? Your strap-on, Beaver?"

Well, wake up, little Susie. Joe and I both just nodded dumbly. Finn had just referred to Joe as "Beaver." And she had not belted him. Or even called him a pig. Toto, we were *so* not in Kansas anymore. Or even Minneapolis, for that matter.

Finn sashayed over with a perfectly mixed Stoli martini for me, and my shiny silicone wonder in a harness for Joe. I gulped my martini indelicately as Finn—or was it June?—went back to fuss in the kitchen. Joe just looked at me, holding up the harness. I shrugged and mouthed, "Why the hell not?"

Joe shrugged in response and headed to the bathroom. I stood up myself and walked over to Finn, who was putting the finishing touches on something that looked and smelled oddly like turkey.

"Looks good. What is it?"

He smiled widely. "Tofurky! At least that's the brand name. And we have mashed red potatoes, organic corn, freshly baked bread . . . "

I had to interrupt. "You baked fucking bread?"

"I said freshly baked bread, honey, I did *not* say I baked fucking bread. Please. I can only work so many miracles. Speaking of which," he said, grinning as he slid his ass up onto the counter, "are we having fun yet? Do I fit the bill?"

I let the air out from between my teeth. "You know, you do. You make June Cleaver look like a wallflower."

"June *was* a wallflower. I figured you could use version 2. 0. I call it 'June meets Marilyn.'"

I stuck my finger in the potatoes, tasting them. Not bad at all. Finn batted at my hands. "Go sit your ass down, woman. I'll serve in a minute."

My ass and I headed back to the table, and I watched as Joe strolled back in, now clearly packing that strap-on under her battered jeans. I was working up quite an appetite.

Finn came, took our plates and brought them back filled to the brim with food, then headed back to the kitchen as Joe started munching. Through a mouthful, she muttered, "Okay, are you going to tell me what's going on here?"

I sighed. "I was saying last night to Finn when we were spacing in front of the tube that it wouldn't be such a bad thing to have June Cleaver to come home to."

She rolled her eyes. "Jeez, girl. Rampant sexism and pop culture worship aside, I'm amazed you had the chutzpah to ask Finn to do this."

I slugged the last of the vodka. "I didn't. The meshuggeneh creature actually suggested you do it first." Joe howled with laughter. "Yeah, that was basically my reaction. But I didn't suggest anything. He did this all on his own."

"Unreal." She wiped her chin. "Yo, June!" she shouted to Finn. "You going to come sit down or what?"

He blithely nibbled at a plate in the kitchen. "No, no, no. A good homemaker doesn't sit at the table, silly. Refill on your drink, Ward?"

"Umm. Sure."

He filled the shaker and shimmied over, and Joe's eyes, watching Finn's hips, clicked back and forth like one of those ridiculous Kit-Kat clocks. This was getting completely out of hand. And I was really losing my interest in dinner. Fuck it. Dinner could wait.

"Finn . . . er, June?"

"Yes, darling?" he said.

"I'm ready for dessert. And you are not going back to the kitchen to get it."

Joe dropped her fork and grinned. "Well, shit. You go, girl."

I was fortified with enough Stoli to feel in charge. "Oh, no. You go, girl. Finn, if you won't sit at the table, sit the hell under it."

Finn looked slightly startled, and more than slightly amused. I looked him square in the face. "Look: Joe told me you looked fuckable, and really, I have to agree. You do look fuckable, and even more fuckable because Joe said it first. Right about now, if I don't get to see some action, I'm going to go out of my mind. So, well . . . yeah. Let's see it. I'm ready."

I moved my chair back to let Finn in under the table, and watched as he got down on his stockinged knees between Joe's legs. My view was imperfect, so I pushed the table out of the way, pulled a smoke from my pocket, lit it and sat back as Joe grabbed Finn's coiffed auburn hair. She ran her finger over his red-patent mouth and looked at me. "Jesus, he looks good."

I nodded. He did look good. So did she. So did the torte on the counter, I'd noticed, but that would keep.

Finn unbuttoned Joe's jeans and slid his mouth over her black silicone appendage, his eyes on me as he swallowed it and pulled his mouth to its tip again. I felt the mashed potatoes melt in my stomach. Then I decided that voyeurism was highly overrated. I slid off my chair and slipped behind Finn on my knees, sliding my hands under his dress, making a beeline to what I knew had to be the erection of the decade. Under silk, no less. Ward Cleaver never had it so good.

He let out a long sigh, and I licked my fingers and slid them up and down his cock as he went down on Joe's dick, the firm silicone smudging his lipstick in a very fetching Joan Crawford-on-a-bender sort of way. I slid the fingers of my other hand around the top of his stocking, reveling in the texture of his leg hair beneath the garters. As he moaned and groaned, I wanted very much to dip my finger into his asshole, but I lacked the proper accoutrements.

"I'll be right back," I whispered in his ear. "I need to go to the bedroom and get—"

He slid a pair of gloves out of one apron pocket and handed them to me, producing a tube of lube from the other pocket. Mama Cleaver certainly did have a brand new bag. I slid on the gloves, enjoying the satisfying pop of latex, lubed them up and let my fingers do the walking.

Joe cocked her head to the side, smiling at me as I circled slowly, then slipped my slick finger into Finn. He cooed, reaching beneath his apron to stroke himself wantonly. I gave Joe a quick wink, but let my eyes wander down to Finn's sweet pucker, watching as my finger slid slowly in and out between the ripe cheeks that protruded from amid the silk and stockings.

I let my other hand wander under Joe's harness straps, working its way beneath her package to wiggle her clit gently. Relishing having both my partners' tender spots in my hands, I pondered pleasantly on what might come next until I realized that if I were going to do half of what I wanted, Finn's apron pockets had better hold what I suspected they might. I slid my hands out from their warm locations and patted Finn's apron pockets. "Hey, June? What else do you have between those apron strings?"

He grinned at me over his shoulder and began unloading his booty. "Why, everything a girl needs, of course! My gloves, my wrap, my hat, my ring and my flask."

I sat silent for a moment, amazed not only with the entire play kit he had tucked in there but by his quick double-entendre. How was it the broad in the Little Black Dress was not only the best dressed, but always the wittiest one in the room?

"Well, that makes it easy," Joe said. "Let's see. Eenie, meenie, minie, mo, catch a tiger by the . . . O!" She picked up the shiny cock ring, grinning. I concurred with a nod. Then we looked at Finn's rather profound erection. Maybe not.

I patted it gently. "Down, boy. Down." It sprang right back up to meet my hand. He shrugged apologetically. Finn was a very bad actor.

Joe shook her head. "I bet he'll be saying he only took his rings off to do the dishes, too, the harlot."

I swerved around Finn and tugged at Joe's jeans. "Well, guess he won't be getting any dessert then. His loss, your gain."

Finn whimpered as I wrestled Joe out of her harness and boxers, unwrapping a dam while she dribbled lube on her twat and spread it around. Sliding the thin sheet of latex over her pussy, I gave a tentative nibble and she slapped her hands to the side of my head. I interpreted this as encouragement and pressed forward, razoring my tongue in long lines between her clit and her hole, pressing her furry chocolate lips rhythmically against my cheeks. As I suckled Joe noisily, Finn's hands slid over my breasts and pushed my dress up to my collarbones, exposing my erect nipples.

I hummed happily into Joe's cunt as Finn pinched my pink nubs, twisting them forcefully between his fingers. Joe teetered slightly in her chair. Finn's hands slithered down over my ribs and my hips, around my thighs, and with a smooth stroke, he pulled my lips back and pressed two fingers hard against my clit. He pulled my ass toward his hips and ground his dick against it as he jiggled my clit. I growled under my breath, and Joe inched back fast with an most un-butch coo and grin.

"Shit, sister," she laughed. "That mouth battery-operated?" I don't think I responded coherently, but I got the point. Clitoral overload was quickly approaching.

"Need a hand?" I managed to mutter.

By way of affirmation, Joe spread her legs wide and leaned back in the chair, arms raised, moaning in anticipation. I managed to slip a new pair of gloves on without disconnecting Finn's fingers from my pulse point, taking in the fine view of her bushy armpits and the dark nipples I could see jutting through her worn top. Her right hand slid to her clit and circled slowly.

Dousing my hands in lube, I slid two fingers into her cunt, twirling them back and forth as Finn moved back and opened a condom, unrolling it unto his cock, seductively whispering in my ear, "Now Ward, don't be too hard on the Beaver." Smartass.

As I worked up to four fingers, tucking my thumb into my palm, Finn's fingers moved back to my clit, twiddling it with evident glee as he circled the tip of his dick over my twat, then pressed in with a long thrust. As he pushed his way into me, I let Joe's cunt swallow the widest part of my hand, reflexively balled up my fist, and churned my wrist in deep as the three of us released a collective squeal.

As we ground rhythmically forward and back, I had a hard time chasing the little voice out of my head that kept gulping and whispering, "Gee Wally, do you think Mom'll be mad?" As if I'd give a rat's ass. And then I felt Joe's cunt start to clench around my hand and swiveled my wrist, watching as she worked her clit manically. I pressed her against the chair with my other hand and drove it home, pulsing my fist open and closed inside her as she growled and shuddered, her juices dripping gorgeously over my glove and down my arm. I barely managed to pull my hand out before she slid off the chair and to her knees in front of me, covering my mouth with hers.

I popped off my gloves and pulled her to me, overwhelmed, all my attention suddenly freed to concentrate on my own body, sandwiched and steaming between lovers. As Finn ground behind me, Joe slid her sticky hands over my hips and nibbled at my neck, reaching for her harness again, buckling herself in, looking to me, then to Finn.

Joe licked her lips and sidled up behind Finn, grinning wolfishly over his shoulder at me as she made her grand entrance. I felt Finn's moan on my back as it rumbled from his stomach; as he arched up behind me, penetrated and penetrating all at once. Lucky boy. I felt the starchy hem of his apron on my ass and smelled Joe's sweet sweat mingled with his and mine. My toes curled as he pumped faster, tapping my clitoris with his fingers like he was drumming out Morse code. I could envision the dildo gyrating, Finn's stocking tops as backdrop, the black straps of the harness over Joe's luxe round brown bottom. The perfect portrait of the American family. In the back of my head the peppy strains of the *Leave it to Beaver* theme song bounced along in time to Finn's tapping fingers and the doubled pounding against my ass.

Then I felt Finn's cock tremble and heard Joe call out, and I came in violent waves, almost giving myself a concussion on the chair I was holding on to for dear life as I thrashed. And as we all moaned, then whimpered, then sighed, then slid unto the floor in a sloppy, drippy pile, my eyes wandered over to Finn, who, despite the smudged lipstick, the unruly coiffure and the dress hiked over his ass, still looked every inch the perfect homemaker.

155

He grinned like an idiot. "Ward, did we handle everything all right?"

I blew air slowly from my lips, smiling. "Bubbe, it was just swell."

"You know, Bella," he teased, "with that head-wrap, and the '70s dress and shoes, you could get a serious Rhoda Morgenstern thing going."

Joe came back from the dead and waved her hands in the air in limp surrender. "Oh, God, no. Even in this trio, no one is perverse enough to wanna fuck Lou Grant."

I waggled an eyebrow and winked at her. "I wouldn't count on it, Beav."

DEAR NICHOLAS

A s I write, the blue sky succumbs to black clouds that eat the horizon, a slow, necessary death. They remind me of you.

Sabine putters. Her mood is one of barely constrained sadness, a calmness tinged with memories since she found the picture. It was buried behind boots and shoes, forgotten in the closet until we did some spring cleaning. If you could see it, would you remember when it was taken? The day the three of us had gone hiking in the mountains and braced the camera on a tree branch in order to capture the moment forever? The freshness of your face, your beautiful smiling face, so happy . . . the last moment in which we would remember you that way. How long has it been? Four years? Five years? Have you forgiven me?

I wonder if you have repressed the memory of when we first met. It's still as fresh to me now as it was that first night. Yours was the first face I'd ever looked into that eradicated the need for words. The people, music, food, drink, at a party neither of us really wanted to be at. The almost undetectable flitting of your eyes from my face to my body. The conversation without words. I remember it all.

I remember the silent ride in the car to the motel room, my eyes tracing the ragged edge of the dark pavement under the heartbeat of streetlights as my hand slithered to your thigh and further, the telling presence of your hard cock under the wool of your suit. The warm wetness on the insides of my thighs when you shut off the engine and we got out of the car.

I remember the moist heat of your hands as they shook against me, popping the buttons of my dress in rapid succession to each breath you rasped against my ear. A thin sliver of dirty yellow light from the motel sign draped your right shoulder as you pulled me to the unfamiliar bed, the bedspread—never turned down in the haste of the moment—smelling of chemicals and the bodies of strangers. I inhaled the heady scent, breathing in your body under me. Still there were no words. I slid down your chest and tasted the thin veneer of salt and cologne that enveloped you with its miniscule sheen, gorging on the meal that was you. I slipped your cock past my lips and listened to you moan in desperate supplication. We fucked, my legs straddling your hips as you locked yourself against me, my fingertips raking the meaty bars of your ribs as my body pushed you further into the bed. And the motel sign bathed us in its unholy aura of depravity.

Somehow without saying so, we both knew it would not be the only time. We did away with the safety and anonymity of sterile motel rooms, opting instead to violate the sanctuary of your bedroom while Sabine was away on business. It was impious, profane, throwing my clothes on the floor and kneeling before you as you sat on the edge of the bed, the sacred altar of your marriage. And the irreverence of it all intoxicated me, empowered me as I felt you hard behind me, my arms resting on the wall, my hips pushing forward and back to fuck you deeper into me.

There were the expected games—whispering "wrong number" when I called and got Sabine instead of you. Leaving cryptic messages with coworkers, as if we were forgotten spies trying to get home.

And then it happened. I met her. Do you remember, Nicholas? I can't imagine you'd forget. We were at a party thrown by mutual employers, forced to network and to promise to do lunch, and you had brought her. I even remember what she wore—black silk pants and jacket, with a sapphire blue linen shirt. Her ears were studded with conservative pearls. I believed, at that moment, that I had never seen a woman until I saw Sabine. And I wondered: *Does she know? Does she taste the traces of me, the heady musk of my pussy, when she sucks your cock in the warm cocoon of the bedroom you fucked me in? Can she feel the grooves my fingernails engrave along your spine as I beg you to go deeper, faster?*

I was angry, Nicholas. From across the room I watched the way your hand settled comfortably in the small of her back as you erupted in deep laughter. I wanted to feel your hand in the small of my back as you forgot that you were putting it there. But as I stood and watched, I realized I would never feel your hand rest casually on my thigh or your fingers press lovingly against my arm. I realized that the only way I could feel you, would ever feel you, was when your body pushed mine hard up against a wall in lecherous desperation while your cock slid into me and you whispered salacious suggestions hoarsely into my ear, or when you twisted my long hair around your hand and pulled not quite gently as you entered me from behind, making me moan and rock against you. I wanted these things, Nicholas, but I also wanted more. I was jealous.

So I formulated the seeds of a plan that began with introducing myself to her. And yes, I saw the slow transformation of your expression from one of hidden edginess to near-maniacal panic as I crossed the room, clearly intent on Sabine. Seconds stretched to infinity between eye contact with Sabine and eye contact with you, and in those infinite seconds, I did not know what I was going to say. Are you surprised? Did you think I plotted the entire course of the rest of your life in my imagination, placing it in a poisoned gift box? Did you think I would hand that box over to your wife with gracious humility?

No. I was as ignorant as you were. I sat beside her and started the journey that led me here. We talked, not stopping except to refill our drinks. Did you know that what was happening was real, that on that night, what began as revenge would transform into friendship, and into love?

It was then that Sabine and I began spending time together. I can still see the look in your eyes when I showed up at your front door to get Sabine so she and I could do our Christmas shopping. The pain in your eyes shot through me, and I couldn't explain the idea, the process, the result, and where it all went wrong.

And yet, there was still you and I. I remember even that night we met at a motel, the same one as the first time, and you pulled me into the deafening, inky darkness of the room, pressing your mouth against mine in anger and lust. You nearly ripped the clothes from my body and pushed me down onto the bed with the same carnal fury as you had all the times before, but this time your lust held a defiant, dangerous edge. I remember it—on my hands and knees, hair falling forward and pooling in a golden, angelic halo over my hands and arms as you fucked me, crashing into me with each movement of your hips as if to fuck me away from Sabine. Is that why we continued, Nicholas? So that you could try, with every thrust of your cock, to distance me from your wife?

It may have been, Nicholas, but she knew. Although I never told her, there was an unspoken haze of sex that surrounded the three of us. And even though I didn't know it at the time, the further you tried to take me from her, the closer we became. It culminated the last night we fucked in your bedroom. It was fitting, really. Did you ever know, Nicholas?

We were on the bed, the darkness of the room surrounding us except for the razor-sharp sliver of hallway light that crept in. The door was open slightly. You had said Sabine was going to be out of town until the next day. You lay under me as I took you in my mouth and began a slow rhythm that matched your breathing. Your fingers tangled in the strands of my hair as they undulated along your stomach, your head tipping back with closed eyes in ecstasy. And then I saw her.

She stood in the doorway, silent, the backlighting of the hallway preventing any glimpse of her expression. But I didn't need to see it. In that moment, the connection between her and me took control of what I was doing. With your head toward the doorway, you were

unaware of her presence. I slid your cock out of my mouth and straddled you, in one movement sliding you past the lips of my pussy and
as deep into me as I could make you go. I saw Sabine's hand go to the
doorframe as if to steady herself, and as I ground my hips against
yours, listening to your moans, I locked eyes with her, refusing to let
her go. I was fucking her through you. I felt it, and I knew she did too,
and that was when I grabbed a handful of your short dark hair and,
pulling your head back, sunk my teeth into your neck, sucking at the
skin. I watched as Sabine's fingertips traced a hardened nipple through
the thin silk of her shirt, saw her lips part slowly to let uneven breath
escape. Again I locked eyes with her, moving my hips faster against
yours and gripping your shoulders with my fingernails. I watched her
breathing time itself to mine. I fucked you and made love to her, and,
without taking my eyes from hers, came in a violent explosion that I
knew she could feel.

She turned toward the light enough for me to see her smile.

Since that night, I have wondered many things. Why Sabine? Before
her, woman was never anything more to me than something in the
mirror. And what was it that drove you from us? Sabine and I both
watched you walk the halls of our lives like a restless ghost, a shadow
that faded further and further from our grasp. You could have stayed,
you know. You were the catalyst for a reaction that none of us understood, but felt all the same. Was it the night you saw Sabine and me in
your bedroom, profaning the sanctity of that stark chamber the same
way you and I did? The way her hands moved over me in blessing, her
voice whispering prayers against my neck while her fingers took holy
water from inside me and, in a baptismal rite, traced the peaks of my
nipples and then licked it from my skin? Was it your relegation to the
role of altar boy that ruined you?

I can live without the answers, Nicholas. We are happy. But I
have often wondered one thing: Can you forgive her for being happy
with me?

Contributor Biographies

L. E. Bland ("The Fourteenth Day") relocated from the Deep South to the Wild West where she discovered all things taboo. She writes nasty stories drawn from her bisexual adventures in the Texas leather scene and in the world of professional perversion. She has been published in *Danzine, Zaftig!: Sex for the Well-Rounded, Faster Pussycats* (Alyson), and online in *Scarlet Letters*. Her work also appears under the name Elise Chapman.

Heather Corinna ("Swell") is the chain-smoking, pug-wrangling bodhisattva who founded and edits the long-running websites scarletletters.com, scarleteen.com and femmerotic.com. Her sexuality art and prose has appeared online in numerous venues since 1997, in her sex information columns at *Technodyke* and *Chickclick*, and in the print anthologies *Viscera, The Adventures of Food, Aqua Erotica, Zaftig: Well Rounded Erotica*, and *The Mammoth Book of Best New Erotica*. A Chicago native, she now lives and works in Minneapolis.

Jaclyn Friedman ("Deeper") is not always a femme fatale, but she *could* kill you. Her work has appeared in *Best Bisexual Erotica, Philogyny, Sojourner*, and the occasional bathroom stall, and she has usurped countless hours of mike time in venues across New England, including a memorable three minutes with the babes of Sister Spit. She writes her dirty stories and aggressively personal poetry in Somerville, MA, where she is the events coordinator for New Words Bookstore and is pursuing an MFA at Emerson College.

R. Gay ("A Cool Dry Place") is a writer slowly starting to feel like she really is a writer. Her work can be found in several anthologies including *Herotica 7, Best Bisexual Women's Erotica, Best Transgender Erotica*, and *Love Shook My Heart II*. Her free time is spent in an English graduate program as she looks forward to law school next year and perhaps finally deciding what she wants to be when she grows up.

Sacchi Green ("To Remember You By") was born in 1943, which may explain her fascination with the World War II era. She figures that, after the first half-century, anyone has a right to multiple lives; she leads hers in western Massachusetts, the mountains of New Hampshire, and her libidinous imagination. Some manifestations of the latter can be read in *Best Women's Erotica 2001* and *2002*, several editions of *Best Lesbian Erotica*, and various other anthologies including *Zaftig: Well Rounded Erotica* and *Best Transgender Erotica*.

Helena Grey ("Perfect") lives on the East coast, studying psychology and spending as much of her free time as possible amid a pile of very good books. She has contributed in the past to web sites concerning issues of disability and sexuality such as www.disabledsex.org.

Adhara Law ("Dear Nicholas") has been writing fiction since she was a little girl, but really got going when she fell into erotica. Now 29 years old, her work has been featured both in print and online, in places such as *Clean Sheets*, *Scarlet Letters*, and in the anthology *Desires*. Her corner of the internet, www.adharalaw.com, contains her fiction, non-fiction, and more. She lives in California with her husband but calls Wyoming her home.

Catherine Lundoff ("Persistence of Memory") lives in Minneapolis with her fabulous partner and kitties. She's a computer geek by day, a writer by night and a member of an anarchist bookstore collective in her spare time. Her fiction has appeared in such science fiction and erotica anthologies as *Such a Pretty Face*, *Zaftig: Well Rounded Erotica*, *Set in Stone: Butch on Butch Erotica*, and *Best Lesbian Erotica 2001*.

Jessica Melusine ("Spark Me") lives and writes in Boston, MA. She is an active Lesbian Avenger and an editrix and writer for butchdykeboy.com. For this story, she salutes alt.gothic, pridegoth-l and the coolest Chigoths, who know just who they are. She sends love and pleasure to her dearest ones near and far.

Lucy Moore ("I Can Still Smell You") is a writer and general ne'er do well whose work has appeared in *Clean Sheets*, *Scarlet Letters*, and other salacious publications. If you need her, she's probably at the beach.

Dawn O'Hara ("Pregnant Pause") has a closet stuffed with dirty stories, but she maintains her only real perversion is writing them down. Her closet is bottomless, but at least the door is now open. Dawn is the uninhibited alter-ego of an outwardly respectable and unassuming tea addict whose credits include *Calyx*, *Hedgebrook*, and winner of Seattle Writers Association essay contest and Redmond Spoken Word fiction contest. She prefers writing smut to reading it. Dawn gave up her Block Watch Hostess crown this year. Contact her at dawno_hara@hotmail.com.

Jean Roberta ("Communion") has had many periods in her first fifty years, and will probably have fewer in the next fifty. She has a grown daughter, two grown stepsons and a long-term partner. She teaches English at a university on the Canadian prairie, and embarrasses her friends and relatives by writing erotica and opinionated editorials.

Former art student **Helena Settimana** ("When We Were One") lives with her partner and cats in Toronto. Her work has appeared in numerous web and print publications including the *Erotica Readers Association* (where she acts as Features Editor), *Clean Sheets*, *Scarlet Letters*, *Best Women's Erotica 2001* and *2002*, *Herotica 7*, *Erotic Travel Tales* and *Best Bisexual Women's Erotica*. When she's not writing, she paints, makes clay sculpture and teaches clay craft to adults.

Simone Temple ("Cages") is the pseudonym of a belly dancing, pseudo-Goth, fashion-fixated chick who lives and works in Seattle with her husband. "Cages" is her first published story. She has just finished her first novel, a tale about a dominatrix who stalks a famous film director, igniting a psychosexual duel that explores the boundaries of gender, sexuality, and self-identity. (Now she just has to come up with a title and a publisher.) She would like to thank the members of the No Safeword Writers' Group and her other writer friends for all their feedback on her work. Reach her at simonetemple@hotmail.com.

Anne Tourney's ("The Book of Zanah") erotic fiction has appeared in various journals and anthologies, including the *Best American Erotica* and *Best Women's Erotica* series, *Zaftig: Well-Rounded Erotica*, *The Unmade Bed*, and the online magazines *Scarlet Letters* and *Clean Sheets*. Her horror fiction has appeared in *Embraces: Dark Erotica and Dark Regions*.

Hua Tsao Mao ("Seven Women") lives on New York's scenic Third Avenue. She has worked as an exhibit builder for a museum, an artist's model, and a bookbinder in a university library, among other things. She refuses to say how much of her fiction is even remotely autobiographical but welcomes speculation as long as it's flattering.

Zonna ("Stone Cold"). She's 41 and living in New Yawk. Can you tell from her accent? You may have seen her stories in anthologies by Alyson Publications (*Skin Deep; Dykes With Baggage; My Lover, My Friend*), Arsenal Press (*Hot & Bothered II and III*), and Black Books (*Tough Girls*). When she isn't writing, she's usually changing her cat's litter box.

About the Editor

Raised in Cleveland, Ohio, and trained as a classical musician and cultural historian, Hanne Blank is a writer, editor, public speaker, activist, and educator whose books include *Best Transgender Erotica* (with Raven Kaldera, Circlet Press), *Zaftig: Well Rounded Erotica* (Cleis Press), and the groundbreaking *Big Big Love: A Sourcebook on Sex for People of Size and Those Who Love Them* (Greenery Press). Her socially progressive, intellectually- and emotionally-engaged approach to sexuality has been characterized as "sophisticated . . . does for sex what feminism does for women: it gives us context." Proud proprietrix of one hell of a variegated resume, Hanne is co-editor (with Heather Corinna) of literary erotica standard-bearer *Scarlet Letters* (scarletletters.com), the former associate editor of the feminist newsmonthly *Sojourner: The Women's Forum*, and has been an educator at institutions including Whitworth College, Tufts University and Brandeis University. Her fiction, essays, reviews, and other writings are published in a wide range of venues, ranging from erotica anthologies, travel magazines, indie newspapers, zines, feminist and Jewish journals, books on music and culture, and beyond. Hanne and her work have been featured on radio and television in the United States, Canada, and the United Kingdom, and she is a frequent public speaker and workshop leader on topics literary, sexual, and otherwise.

Hanne Blank lives near Baltimore, Maryland. She also maintains an outpost at www.hanne.net where you may, if you wish, find out more.

Selected Seal Press Titles

Sex and Single Girls: Straight and Queer Women on Sexuality edited by Lee Damsky. $16.95, 1-58005-038-7. In this potent and entertaining collection of essays, women lay bare pleasure, fear, desire, risk—all that comes with exploring their sexuality.

Listen Up: Voices from the Next Feminist Generation
edited by Barbara Findlen. $16.95, 1-58005-054-9. The voices of today's young feminists are brought together to explore and reveal their lives.

Body Outlaws:
Young Women Write About Body Image and Identity
edited by Ophira Edut. $14.95, 1-58005-043-3. Essays filled with honesty and humor by women who have chosen to ignore, subvert or redefine the dominant beauty standard.

Young Wives' Tales: New Adventures in Love and Partnership edited by Jill Corral and Lisa Miya-Jervis, foreword by bell hooks. $16.95, 1-58005-050-6. This bold and provocative anthology captures the wide range of responses and lived realities of young women, whether they are trying on the title "wife," deciding who will wear the gown in a lesbian wedding or demanding the space for solitude in a committed relationship.

The Mother Trip:
Hip Mama's Guide to Staying Sane in the Chaos of Motherhood by Ariel Gore. $14.95, 1-58005-029-8. In a book that is part self-help, part critique of the mommy myth and part hip-mama handbook, Ariel Gore offers support to mothers who break the mold.

Breeder: Real-Life Stories from the New Generation of Mothers
edited by Ariel Gore and Bee Lavender, foreword by Dan Savage. $16.00, 1-58005-051-4. From the editors of Hip Mama, this hilarious and heartrending compilation creates a space where Gen-X moms can dish, cry, scream and laugh.